'I'd have given anything to have written *Wasp*. I can't imagine a funnier terrorists' handbook'   Terry Pratchett

SF MASTERWORKS

Wasp

ERIC FRANK RUSSELL

Text copyright © Thomas Bouregy & Company 1957
Introduction copyright © Lisa Tuttle 2012
All rights reserved

The right of Eric Frank Russell to be identified as the author
of this work, and the right of Lisa Tuttle to be identified
as the author of the introduction, has been asserted by
them in accordance with the Copyright, Designs and
Patents Act 1988.

This edition first published in Great Britain in 2013
by Gollancz
An imprint of the Orion Publishing Group
Orion House, 5 Upper St Martin's Lane,
London WC2H 9EA
An Hachette UK Company

3 5 7 9 10 8 6 4 2

A CIP catalogue record for this book
is available from the British Library

ISBN 978 0 575 12904 7

Typeset at The Spartan Press Ltd,
Lymington, Hants

Printed and bound in Great Britain
by Clays Ltd, St Ives plc

The Orion Publishing Group's policy is to use papers that
are natural, renewable and recyclable products and made
from wood grown in sustainable forests. The logging and
manufacturing processes are expected to conform to the
environmental regulations of the country of origin.

www.orionbooks.co.uk
www.gollancz.co.uk

INTRODUCTION

With his laconic, hard-boiled style and regular appearances in the pulp magazines edited by John W. Campbell, Eric Frank Russell was assumed by many readers to be an American writer, but in fact he was thoroughly British: born into a military family in 1905, he spent his youth in England, Egypt and the Sudan. During the Second World War he served in the RAF, and he worked as an engineer before becoming a full-time writer.

His strong scientific interests led him to science fiction, of which he was soon an active fan. Along with Arthur C. Clarke and Ted Carnell, Russell was one of the original members of the British Interplanetary Society, formed in 1933, and went to the first ever science fiction convention, at the Theosophical Hall in Leeds on 3 January 1937. This one-day event was attended by about twenty people, but also received messages of support and encouragement from such luminaries as H. G. Wells, Olaf Stapledon, John Russell Fearn and Festus Pragnell.

Russell's first published story, 'The Saga of Pelican West', appeared in the February 1937 issue of *Astounding Science Fiction*, and he went on to become a mainstay of that magazine until he gave up writing sometime in the late 1960s. Critics are generally agreed that much of his best work was written in the 1950s, including the Hugo Award-winning short story 'Alamagoosa' (1955) and his 1957 novel *Wasp*.

The significance of the title, and indeed the general idea of the book, is explained near the beginning, in a description of an accident caused by a driver's distraction as he attempted to swat an insect: 'The weight of a wasp is under half an ounce. Compared with a human being, the wasp's size is minute, its strength negligible. Its sole armament is a tiny syringe holding a drop of irritant, formic acid. In this instance, the wasp didn't use it. Nevertheless, that wasp killed four big men and converted a large, powerful car into a heap of scrap.'

James Mowry, the hero of this book, is enlisted by his government to be the intrusive 'wasp' who may help the human race win a war against the Sirian Empire. Disguised as one of the purple-skinned aliens, armed only with a printer, a nearly infinite supply of counterfeit money, and his own wits, his mission is to sow confusion and fear, to distract the Sirians from battle by inducing them to pour more energy into a futile fight against an imaginary internal threat. A few stickers proclaiming the existence of a well-organized underground anti-war movement starts the ball rolling; paranoia among the Sirian top brass does the rest.

Wasp is classic 'Golden Age' SF – the sort of book that, read at the right time, stays with the reader forever. But even if your own golden age (11, or 14, or even older) is long gone, it can still be read with enjoyment. Don't expect great characterization – the hero, one of the breed of 'ordinary' yet supremely competent men so admired by John W. Campbell Jr, is barely sketched, and there's even less substance to the other figures in the landscape. Plot and style are similarly serviceable. What remains, and what makes *Wasp* such an entertaining and thought-provoking read, is the idea, and the vigour, inventiveness and wry humour with which that idea is explored through a briskly paced series of events.

It would make a great movie, and would surely have been one by now if not for the bitter sting in its tail. For this clever, funny and compelling story could be described as a celebration of terrorism – possibly even a terrorist's handbook. The reader can't help cheering on the hero, delighting in his success. The fact that he is a human being pitted against aliens doesn't change much, for the Sirians differ from humans in only a few small details (purple skin, pinned-back ears, a bow-legged walk), and if most of those Mowry encounters are stupid bureaucrats or criminal thugs, so are the other human beings he must deal with. Russell, who wrote some fine anti-war stories, was surely well aware of the moral ambiguity of this tale.

In 1970, motion picture rights to *Wasp* were bought by The Beatles' Apple Corporation, but the film was never made. Three decades on, Neil Gaiman bought an option and began to write the script. He had not got very far by September 11, 2001, and subsequently let the option expire, feeling that it would be a very long time before anyone, especially in America, was ready for a terrorist hero.

That may still be true, yet, in the world we live in now, where impossible levels of security are routinely demanded, at huge cost to us all, *Wasp* may serve as a timely reminder of the dangers of blinkered thinking and over-reaction. A wasp can sting, and someone who is stung may die from anaphylactic shock, but do you have to go into lock-down mode, or torch your own house, if a wasp gets in? Terrorists are not the only threat we face – and sometimes, laughter is the best response.

Lisa Tuttle

ONE

He ambled into the room, sat in the indicated chair, and said nothing. The baffled expression had been on his face for some time and he was getting a bit tired of wearing it.

The big fellow who had brought him all the way from Alaska now departed, silently closing the door and leaving him alone with the man contemplating him from behind the desk. A small plaque on the desk informed him that this character's name was William Wolf. It was inappropriate; the man looked more like a bull moose.

Wolf said in hard, even tones, 'Mr Mowry, you are entitled to an explanation.' There was a pause, followed by, 'You will get one.' Then Wolf stared unblinkingly at his listener.

For a long-drawn minute James Mowry suffered the intent scrutiny before he asked, 'When?'

'Soon.'

With that, Wolf went on staring. Mowry found the gaze unpleasantly piercing, analytical; and the face around it seemed to be as warm and expressive as a lump of hard rock.

'Mind standing up?'

Mowry stood up.

'Turn around.'

He rotated, looking bored.

'Walk to and fro across the room.'

He walked.

'Tsk-tsk!' grunted Wolf in a way that indicated neither

pleasure nor pain. 'I assure you, Mr Mowry, that I am quite serious when I ask you to oblige by walking bow-legged.'

Mowry stumped around as if riding an invisible horse. Then he resumed his chair and said pointedly, 'There had better be money in this. I don't come three thousand miles and perform like a clown for nothing.'

'There's no money in it, not a cent,' said Wolf. 'If you're lucky, there is life.'

'And if I'm out of luck?'

'Death.'

'You're damnably frank about it,' Mowry commented.

'In this job I have to be.' Wolf stared at him again, long and penetratingly. 'You'll do. Yes, I'm sure you'll do.'

'Do for what?'

'I'll tell you in a moment.' Opening a drawer, Wolf extracted some papers and passed them over. 'These will enable you to understand the situation better. Read them through – they lead up to what follows.'

Mowry glanced at them. They were typed copies of press reports. Settling back in his chair, he perused them slowly.

The first told of a prankster in Roumania. This fellow had done nothing more than stand in the road and gaze fascinatedly at the sky, occasionally crying, 'Blue flames!' Curious people had joined him and gaped likewise. The group became a crowd; the crowd became a mob.

Soon the audience blocked the street and overflowed into side streets. Police tried to break it up, making matters worse. Some fool summoned the fire squads. Hysterics on the fringes swore they could see, or had seen, something weird above the clouds. Reporters and cameramen rushed to the scene; rumours raced around. The government sent up the air force for a closer look and panic spread over an area of two hundred square miles, from which the original cause had judiciously disappeared.

'Amusing if nothing else,' remarked Mowry.

'Read on.'

The second report concerned a daring escape from jail. Two notorious killers had stolen a car; they made six hundred miles before recapture, fourteen hours later.

The third report detailed an automobile accident: three killed, one seriously injured, the car a complete wreck. The sole survivor had died nine hours later.

Mowry handed back the papers. 'What's all this to me?'

'We'll take those reports in order, as read,' began Wolf. 'They prove something of which we've been long aware but which you may not have realized. Now, let's take the first one. That Roumanian did nothing, positively nothing, except stare at the sky and mumble. Yet he forced a government to start jumping around like fleas on a hot griddle. It shows that in given conditions, action and reaction can be ridiculously out of proportion. By doing insignificant things in suitable circumstances, one can obtain results monstrously in excess of the effort.'

'I'll grant you that,' Mowry conceded.

'Now consider the two convicts. They didn't do much, either. They climbed a wall, seized a car, drove like mad until the gas ran out, then got caught.' Wolf leaned forward and continued with added emphasis, 'But for the better part of fourteen hours, they monopolized the attention of six planes, ten helicopters, one hundred and twenty patrol-cars. They tied up eighteen telephone exchanges, uncountable phone lines and radio link-ups, not to mention police, deputies, posses of volunteers, hunters, trackers, forest rangers and National Guardsmen. The total was twenty-seven thousand, scattered over three states.'

'Phew!' Mowry raised his eyebrows.

'Finally, let's consider this auto smash-up. The survivor was able to tell us the cause before he died. He said the driver lost control at high speed while swiping at a wasp which had flown in through a window and was buzzing around his face.'

'It nearly happened to me once.'

Ignoring that, Wolf said, 'The weight of a wasp is under

half an ounce. Compared with a human being, the wasp's size is minute, its strength negligible. Its sole armament is a tiny syringe holding a drop of irritant, formic acid. In this instance, the wasp didn't use it. Nevertheless, that wasp killed four big men and converted a large, powerful car into a heap of scrap.'

'I see the point, but where do I come in?'

'Right here,' said Wolf. 'We want you to become a wasp.'

Leaning back, James Mowry eyed the other man contemplatively. 'The muscle-bound lug who brought me here was a Secret Service agent who had satisfied me as to the genuineness of his credentials. This is a government department. You're a high-ranking official. But for those facts, I'd say you're crazy.'

'Maybe I am,' replied Wolf, blank-faced, 'but I don't think so.'

'You want me to do something?'

'Yes.'

'Something extra-special?'

'Yes.'

'At risk of death?'

'I'm afraid so.'

'And for no reward?'

'Correct.'

Mowry stood up. 'I'm not crazy, either.'

'You will be,' said Wolf, in the same flat tones, 'if you rest content to let the Sirians kick us out of existence.'

Mowry sat down again. 'What d'you mean?'

'There's a war on.'

'I know. Everybody knows.' Mowry made a disparaging gesture. 'We've been fighting the Sirian Combine for ten months. The newspapers, radio, video and government all say so. I am credulous enough to believe the lot of them.'

'Then perhaps you're willing to stretch your credulity a bit further and swallow a few more items,' Wolf suggested.

'Such as?'

'The Terran public is complacent because, to date, nothing

4

has happened in this sector. They know that the enemy has launched two determined attacks against our solar system and that both have been beaten off. The public has great confidence in Terran defences. That confidence is justified. No Sirian task force will ever penetrate this far.'

'Well then – what have we to worry about?'

'Wars must be won or lost. There's no other alternative. We cannot win merely by keeping the foe at arm's length. We can never gain victory solely by postponing defeat.' Suddenly and emphatically, Wolf slammed a heavy fist on his desk and made a pen leap two feet into the air. 'We've got to do more than that. We've *got* to seize the initiative and get the enemy flat on his back while we beat the devil out of him.'

'But we'll get around to that in due course, won't we?'

'Maybe,' said Wolf, 'and maybe not. It depends.'

'Depends upon what?'

'Whether we make full and intelligent use of our resources, especially people – meaning people such as you.'

'You could be more specific,' Mowry suggested.

'Look . . . in technical matters we are ahead of the Sirian Combine – a little ahead in some respects and far ahead in others. That gives us the advantage of better weapons, and more efficient armaments. But what the public does not know – because nobody has seen fit to tell them – is that the Sirians also have an advantage. They outnumber us by twelve to one and outweigh us by material in the same proportion.'

'Is that a fact?'

'Unfortunately it is, though our propagandists don't bother to mention it. Our war-potential is superior qualitatively. The Sirians have superiority quantitatively. That's a very serious handicap to us. We've got to counter it in the best way we know how. It won't be done by playing for time while we make the effort to overtake and surpass their population.'

'I see.' James Mowry gnawed his bottom lip and looked thoughtful.

'However,' Wolf went on, 'the problem becomes less

5

formidable than it looks if we bear in mind that one man can shake a government, two men temporarily can pin down an army twenty-seven thousand strong, or one small wasp can slay four comparative giants and destroy their huge machine into the bargain.' He paused, watching Mowry for effect, then continued, 'Which means that by scrawling suitable words upon a wall, the right man in the right place at the right time might immobilize an armoured division.'

'That's a pretty unorthodox form of warfare.'

'So much the better.'

'I am sufficiently perverse to like such methods. They appeal to me.'

'We know,' said Wolf. He took a file from his desk, and thumbed through it. 'Upon your fourteenth birthday you were fined one hundred Sirian guilders for expressing your opinion of an official, upon a wall, in letters twenty inches high. Your father apologized on your behalf and pleaded the impetuosity of youth. The Sirians were annoyed, but let the matter drop.'

'Razaduth was a scheming, potbellied liar and I say it again.' Mowry eyed the file. 'Is that my life story there?'

'Yes.'

'Nosy lot aren't you?'

'We have to be. We regard it as part of the price to be paid for survival.' Shoving the file to one side, Wolf informed him, 'We've a punched card for every Terran in existence. In no time worth mentioning, we can sort out electronically all those who have false teeth, or wear size eleven shoes, or had red-haired mothers, or can be relied upon to try to dodge the draft. Without trouble we can extract any specified type of sheep from the general mass of sheep and goats.'

'And I am a specified sheep?'

'Speaking metaphorically, of course. No insult is intended.' Wolf's face made a craggy twitch, apparently the nearest it could come to a smile. 'We first dug out about sixteen thousand fluent speakers of the several Sirian dialects. Eliminating the females and children brought the number down to nine thousand.

6

Then, step by step, we cut out the elderly, the infirm, the weak, the untrustworthy, and the temperamentally unsuitable. We weeded out those too short, too tall, too fat, too thin, too stupid, too rash, too cautious, and so forth. We weren't left with many among whom to seek for wasps.'

'What defines a wasp?'

'Several things – but mostly a short man who can walk slightly bandy-legged, with his ears pinned back, and his face dyed purple. In other words, one who can play the part of a native-born Sirian and do it well enough to fool the Sirians.'

'Never!' exclaimed Mowry. 'Never in a month of Sundays! I'm pink, I've got wisdom teeth, and my ears stick out.'

'The surplus teeth can be pulled. Surgical removal of a sliver of cartilage will fasten your ears back good and tight, leaving no visible evidence of the operation. It's painless and easy, and will heal completely in two weeks. That is medical evidence, so don't argue it.' Again the craggy twitch. 'As for the purple complexion, it's nothing startling. There are some Terrans who are a good deal more purple-faced than any Sirian, having acquired the colour via many gallons of booze. We have a dye guaranteed for four months, and a retinting kit that will enable you to carry on as much longer as may be necessary.'

'But . . .'

'Listen to me. You were born in Masham, capital city of Diracta – the Sirian home planet. Your father was a trader there at the time. You lived on Diracta until the age of seventeen, when you returned with your parents to Terra. Luckily you happen to be just about Sirian size and build. You are now twenty-six and still speak perfect Sirian, with a decided Mashambi accent – which, if anything, is an advantage. It lends plausibility. About fifty million Sirians speak with Mashambi accents. You're a natural for the job we have in mind.'

'What if I invite you to thrust the job right up the air shaft?' asked Mowry, with great interest.

'I would regret it,' said Wolf coldly, 'because in time of war it is an old, well-founded adage that one volunteer is worth a thousand conscripts.'

'Meaning I'd get my call-up papers?' Mowry made a gesture of irritation. 'Damn! – I'd rather walk into something of my own accord than be frogmarched into it.'

'So it says here in the file. James Mowry, twenty-six, restless and pigheaded. Can be trusted to do anything at all – provided the alternative is worse.'

'You sound like my father. Did he tell you that?'

'The Service does not reveal its sources of information.'

'Humph!' Mowry pondered a little while, then asked, 'Suppose I volunteer? What follows?'

'We'll send you to a school. It runs a special course that is fast and tough, and takes six to eight weeks. You'll be crammed to the gills with everything likely to be useful to you: weapons, explosives, sabotage, propaganda, psychological warfare, map reading, compass reading, camouflage, judo, radio techniques, and maybe a dozen other subjects. By the time they've finished with you, you'll be fully qualified to function as a complete and absolute pain-in-the-neck.'

'And after that?'

'You will be dropped surreptitiously upon a Sirian-held planet and be left to make yourself as irritating as possible.'

There was a lengthy silence, at the end of which Mowry admitted grudgingly, 'Once when my father was thoroughly irritated, he said, "Son, you were born a fool and you'll die a fool." ' He released a long, deep sigh. 'The old man was dead right. I hereby volunteer.'

'We knew you would,' said Wolf imperturbably.

He saw Wolf again two days after he had finished the arduous course and passed with satisfactory marks. Wolf arrived at the school and visited James Mowry in his room.

'What was it like?'

'Sheer sadism,' said Mowry, making a face. 'I'm beaten up in mind and body. I feel like a half-stunned cripple.'

'You'll have plenty of time to get over that. The journey will take long enough. You're leaving Thursday.'

'For where?'

'Sorry – I can't tell you. Your pilot carries sealed orders, to be opened only on the last lap. In case of accident or successful interception, he destroys them unread.'

'What's the likelihood of our being captured on the way there?'

'Not great. Your ship will be considerably faster than anything the enemy possesses. But even the best of vessels can get into trouble once in a while, so we're taking no chances. You know the reputation of the Sirian Security Police, the Kaitempi. They can make a slab of granite confess its crimes. Should they snatch you *en route* and learn your intended destination, they'd take counter-measures to trap your successor on arrival.'

'My successor? That raises a question nobody here seems willing to answer. Maybe you can tell me, huh?'

'What is it?' asked Wolf.

'Will I be entirely on my own, or will other Terrans be operating on the same planet? If there will be others, how shall I make contact?'

'So far as you're concerned, you'll be the only Terran for a hundred million miles around,' replied Wolf. 'You will have no contacts, so you won't be able to betray anyone to the Kaitempi. Nothing they can do will extract from you information that you don't possess.'

'That would sound better if you didn't smack your lips over the horrid prospect,' reproved Mowry. 'Anyway, it would be some comfort and encouragement to know that other wasps are similarly active, even if there's only one to a planet.'

'You didn't go through this course alone, did you? The others weren't here merely to provide company for you.' Wolf held out a hand. 'Good hunting, be a curse to the foe – *and come back.*'

'I shall return,' sighed Mowry, 'though the way be flinty and the road be long.'

That, he thought as Wolf departed, was more of a pious hope than a performable promise. Indeed, the remark about 'your successor' showed that losses had been anticipated and steps taken to provide replacements.

It occurred to Mowry then that perhaps his own status was that of somebody else's successor. Maybe on the world to which he was going, some unlucky wasp had been trapped and pulled apart very slowly. If so, the Kaitempi might be watching the skies right now, licking their chops in anticipation of their next victim – one James Mowry, twenty-six, restless and pig-headed.

Oh, well, he had committed himself and there was no backing out. It looked as if he was doomed to become a hero from sheer lack of courage to be a coward. Slowly he developed a philosophic resignation which still possessed him, several weeks later, when the corvette's captain summoned him to the mid-cabin.

'Sleep well?'

'Not in the last spell,' Mowry admitted. 'The propulsors were noisier than usual; the whole ship shuddered and creaked.'

The captain gave a wry smile. 'You didn't know it, but we were being chased by four Sirian destroyers. We hit up top speed and lost them.'

'You sure they aren't still tracking us?'

'They've fallen behind range of our detectors; therefore we're beyond range of theirs.'

'Thank heavens for that,' said Mowry.

'I've opened the orders. We're due to arrive in forty-eight Earth-hours.'

'Where?'

'On a planet called Jaimec. Ever heard of it?'

'Yes, the Sirian news channels used to mention it every once in a while. It's one of their outpost worlds, if I remember rightly – underpopulated and not half-developed. I never met anyone from there and so I don't know much about it.' He registered mild annoyance. 'This secretiveness is all very well, but it would help a fellow some to let him know where he's going, and give him some useful information about the place before he gets there.'

'You'll land with all the data we've got,' soothed the captain. 'They've supplied a stack of information with the orders.' He put a wad of papers on the table, along with several maps and a number of large photographs. Then he pointed to a cabinet standing against a wall. 'That's the stereoscopic viewer. Use it to search these pics for a suitable landing place. The choice is wholly yours. My job is to put you down safely wherever you choose and get away undetected.'

'How long have I got?'

'You must show me the selected spot not later than forty hours from now.'

'And how long can you allow for dumping me and my equipment?'

'Twenty minutes maximum. Positively no more. I'm sorry about that, but it can't be helped. If we sit on the ground, and take it easy, we'll leave unmistakable signs of our landing – a whacking big rut that can soon be spotted by air patrols and will get the hunt after you in full cry. So we'll have to use the antigravs and move fast. The antigravs soak up power. Twenty minutes' output is the most we can afford.'

'All right.' Mowry shrugged in resignation, took up the papers, and started reading them as the captain went out.

Jaimec, ninety-fourth planet of the Sirian Empire. Mass seven-eighths that of Terra. Land area about half that of Terra's, the rest being ocean. First settled two and a half centuries ago. Present population estimated at about eighty millions. Jaimec had cities, railroads, spaceports, and all the other features of alien civilization. Nevertheless, much of it remained undeveloped, unexplored, and in primitive condition.

James Mowry plunged into a meticulous study of the planet's surface as shown in the stereoscopic viewer. By the fortieth hour, he had made his choice. It had not been easy to reach a decision; every seemingly suitable landing place had some kind of disadvantage, proving that the ideal hide-out does not exist. One would be beautifully positioned from the strategic viewpoint, but would lack adequate cover. Another would have first-class natural concealment but dangerous location.

The captain came in saying, 'I hope you've picked a point on the night-side. If it isn't, we'll have to dodge around until dark and that's not good. The best technique is to go in and get out before they've time to take alarm and organize a counter-blow.'

'This is it.' Mowry indicated the place on a photo. 'It's a lot farther from a road than I'd have liked – about twenty miles, and all of it through virgin forest. Whenever I need something out of the cache it will take me a day's hard going to reach it, maybe two days. But by the same token it should remain safe from prying eyes, and that's the prime consideration.'

Sliding the photo into the viewer, the captain switched on the interior lighting and looked into the rubber eyepiece. He frowned with concentration. 'You mean that marked spot on the cliff?'

'No – it's at the cliff's base. See that outcrop of rock? What's a fraction north of it?'

The captain stared again. 'It's hard to tell for certain, but it looks mighty like a cave formation.' He backed off, picked up the intercom phone. 'Hame, come here, will you?'

Hamerton, the chief navigator, arrived, studied the photo, and found the indicated point. He compared it with a two-hemisphere map of Jaimec and made swift calculations. 'We'll catch it on the night-side, but only by the skin of our teeth.'

'You sure of that?' asked the captain.

'If we went straight there, we'd make it with a couple of hours to spare. But we daren't go straight – their radar network would plot the dropping point to within half a mile. So we'll have to dodge around below their radar horizon. Evasive action takes time, but with luck we can complete the drop half an hour before sunrise.'

'Let's go straight there,' prompted Mowry. 'It will cut your risks and I'm willing to take a chance on being nabbed. I'm taking the chance, anyway, am I not?'

'Nuts to that,' retorted the captain. 'We're so close that their detectors are tracking us already. We're picking up their identification calls and we can't answer, not knowing their code. Pretty soon it will sink into their heads that we're hostile. They'll send up a shower of proximity-fused missiles, as usual too late. The moment we dive below their radar horizon, they'll start a full-scale aerial search covering five hundred miles around the point where we disappeared.' He frowned at Mowry. 'And you, chum, would be dead centre of that circle.'

'It looks as if you've done this job a few times before,' prompted Mowry, hoping for a revealing answer.

The captain continued, 'Once we're running just above treetop level, they can't track us with radar. So we'll duck down a couple of thousand miles from your dropping point and make for there on a cockeyed course. It's my responsibility to dump you where you want to be put, without betraying you to the whole world. If I don't succeed, the entire trip has been wasted. Leave this to me, will you?'

'Sure,' agreed Mowry, abashed. 'Anything you say.'

They went out, leaving him to brood. Presently the alarm gong clanged upon the cabin wall. He grabbed handholds and hung on while the ship made a couple of violent swerves, first one way, then the other. He could see nothing and hear nothing save the dull moan of steering-jets; but his imagination pictured a cluster of fifty ominous vapour-trails rising from below – fifty long, explosive cylinders eagerly sniffing around for the scent of alien metal.

Eleven more times the alarm sounded, followed at once by aerial acrobatics. By now, the ship resounded to the soft whistle of passing atmosphere which built up to a faint howl as it thickened.

Getting near now.

Mowry gazed absently at his fingers. They were steady, but sweaty. There were queer electric thrills running up and down his spine. His knees felt weak, and his stomach felt weaker.

Far across the void was a planet with a fully comprehensive card-system; and because of that, James Mowry was about to have his pointed head shoved into the lion's mouth. Mentally he damned card-systems, and those who'd invented them, and those who operated them.

By the time propulsion ceased, and the ship stood silently upon its antigravs above the selected spot, he had generated the fatalistic impatience of a man facing a major operation that no longer can be avoided. He half-ran, half-slid down the nylon ladder to the ground. A dozen of the corvette's crew followed, equally in a hurry but for different reasons. They worked like maniacs, all the time keeping a wary eye upon the sky.

TWO

The cliff was part of a plateau rising four hundred feet above the forest. At its bottom were two caves, one wide and shallow, one narrow but deep. Before the caves stretched a beach of tiny pebbles; at its edge a small stream swirled and bubbled.

Cylindrical duralumin containers, thirty in all, were lowered from the ship's belly to the beach, seized and carried to the back of the deep cave, stacked so that the code numbers on their lids faced the light. That done, the twelve crewmen scrambled monkeylike up the ladder, which was promptly reeled in. An officer waved a hand from the open lock and shouted, 'Give 'em hell, Sonny.'

The corvette's tail snorted, making trees wave their tops in a mile-long lane of superheated air. That added to the list of possible risks; if the leaves were scalded – if they withered and changed colour – a scouting airplane would see a gigantic arrow pointing to the cave. But this was a chance that had to be taken. With swiftly increasing speed, the big vessel went away, keeping low and turning to follow the valley northward.

Watching the ship depart, James Mowry knew that it would not head straight for home. First the crew would take added chances for his sake by zooming in plain view over a number of cities and military strongholds. With luck, this tactic might persuade the enemy that the ship was engaged in photographic reconnaissance, rather than surreptitious landing of personnel.

The testing time would come during the long hours of daylight, and already dawn was breaking to one side. Systematic aerial search in the vicinity would prove that the enemy's suspicions had been aroused in spite of the corvette's misleading antics. The absence of a visible search would not prove the contrary, because, for all Mowry knew, the hunt might be going on elsewhere.

Full light would be needed for his trek through the forest, the depths of which were dark even at midday. While waiting for the sun to rise, he sat on a boulder and gazed in the direction in which the ship had gone. He wouldn't have that captain's job, he decided, for a sack of diamonds. And probably the captain wouldn't have Mowry's for two sacks.

After an hour he entered the cave, opened a container and drew from it a well-worn leather case of indisputable Sirian manufacture. There'd be no sharp eyes noting something foreign-looking about that piece of luggage; it was his own property, purchased in Masham, on Diracta, many years ago.

Making an easy jump across the little stream, he went into the forest and headed westward, frequently checking his direction with the aid of a pocket compass. The going proved rough – but not difficult; the forest was not a jungle. Trees grew large and close together, forming a canopy that shut out all but occasional glimpses of the sky. Luckily, the undergrowth was sparse; one could walk with ease and at a fast pace, provided one took care not to fall over projecting roots. In addition, as he soon realized, progress was helped quite a bit by the fact that, on Jaimec, James Mowry's weight was reduced by nearly twenty pounds, his luggage lighter in the same proportion.

Two hours before sunset he reached the road, having covered twenty miles. He'd made one stop for a meal, and many brief pauses to consult the compass. Behind a roadside tree he upended the case, sat on it, and enjoyed fifteen minutes' rest before making a wary survey of the road. So far, he'd heard no planes or scout-ships snooping overhead, nor was there any abnormal activity upon the road. In fact, during his wait nothing passed along the road in either direction.

Refreshed by the pause, he brushed dirt and leaves from his shoes and trousers, reknotted his typical neck-scarf as only a Sirian could knot it, then examined himself in a steel mirror. His Earth-made copy of Sirian clothes would pass muster; he had no doubt of that. His purple face, pinned-back ears, and Mashambi accent would be equally convincing. But his greatest protection would be the mental block in every Sirian's mind: they wouldn't suspect that an Earthman was masquerading as a Sirian because the idea was too ridiculous to contemplate.

Satisfied that he fitted his rôle, Mowry emerged from the shelter of the trees, walked boldly across the road, and from the other side made a careful study of his exit from the forest. It was essential that he be able to remember it speedily and accurately. The forest was the screen of camouflage around his bolt-hole and there was no telling when he might need to dive into it in a hurry.

Fifty yards farther along the road stood an especially tall tree with a peculiarly wrapped growth around its trunk, and a very gnarly branch formation. He fixed it firmly in his mind; and for good measure, he carried a tablet-shaped slab of stone onto the grass verge and stood it upright beneath the tree.

The result suggested a lonely grave. He stared at the stone and with no trouble at all could imagine words inscribed upon it: *James Mowry – Terran. Strangled by the Kaitempi.*

Dismissing ugly thoughts about the Kaitempi, he started trudging along the road, his gait suggesting a slight bowlegged-ness. From now on, he must be wholly a Sirian named Shir Agavan. Agavan was a forestry surveyor employed by the Jaimec Ministry of Natural Resources, therefore a government official and exempt from military service. Or he could be anyone else, so long as he remained plainly and visibly a Sirian and could produce the papers to prove it.

He moved quickly while the sun sank toward the horizon. He was going to thumb a ride; he wanted one with the minimum of delay, but also he wanted to pick it up as far as possible from the point where he'd left the forest. Like everyone else, Sirians had tongues; they talked. Others listened, and some hard-faced characters had full-time jobs of listening, putting two and two together, and without undue strain arriving at four. His chief peril came from overactive tongues and alert ears.

More than a mile had been covered before two dynocars and one gas truck passed him in quick succession, all going the opposite way. None of the occupants favoured him with more than a perfunctory glance. Another mile went by before anything came in his own direction. This was another gas truck, a big, dirty, lumbering monstrosity that wheezed and grunted as it rolled along.

He waved it down, putting on an air of arrogant authority that never failed to impress all Sirians except those with more arrogance and authority. The truck stopped jerkily and with a tailward boost of fumes; it was loaded with about twenty tons of edible roots. Two Sirians looked down at the pedestrian from the cab. They were unkempt, their clothes baggy and soiled.

'I am of the government,' declared Mowry, with the right degree of importance. 'I wish a ride into town.'

The nearest one opened the door, moved closer to the driver, and made room. Mowry climbed up and squeezed into the seat; it was a close fit for three. He held his case on his knees. The truck emitted a loud bang and lurched forward while the Sirian in the middle gazed dully at the case.

'You are a Mashamban, I think,' ventured the driver.

'Correct. Seems we can't open our mouths without betraying the fact.'

'I have never been to Masham,' continued the driver, using the singsong accents peculiar to Jaimec. 'I would like to go there someday. It is a great place.' He switched to his fellow Sirian. 'Isn't it, Snat?'

'Yar,' said Snat, still mooning at the case.

'Besides, Masham or anywhere on Diracta should be a lot safer than here. And perhaps I'd have better luck there. It has been a stinking bad day. Hasn't it, Snat?'

'Yar,' said Snat.

'Why?' asked Mowry.

'This *soko* of a truck has broken down three times since dawn, and it has stuck in the bog twice. The last time we had to empty it to get it out, and then refill it. With the load we've got, that is work. Hard work.' He spat out the window. 'Wasn't it, Snat?'

'Yar,' said Snat.

'Too bad,' Mowry sympathized.

'As for the rest, you know of it,' said the driver, irefully. 'It has been a bad day.'

'I know of what?' Mowry prompted.

'The news.'

'I have been in the woods since sun-up. One does not hear news in the woods.'

'The ten-time radio announced an increase in the war tax. As if we aren't paying enough. Then the twelve-time radio said a Spakum ship had been zooming around. They had to admit it, because the ship was fired upon from a number of places. We are not deaf when guns fire, nor blind when the target is visible.' He nudged his fellow. 'Are we, Snat?'

'Nar,' confirmed Snat.

'Just imagine that – a lousy Spakum ship sneaking around over our very rooftops. You know what *that* means: they are seeking targets for bombing. Well, I hope none of them get through. I hope every Spakum that heads this way runs straight into a breakup barrage.'

'So do I,' said Mowry. He gave his neighbour a dig in the ribs. 'Don't you?'

'Yar,' said Snat.

For the rest of the journey, the driver maintained his paean of anguish about the general vileness of the day; the iniquity of truck-builders; the menace and expense of war; and the blatant impudence of an enemy ship that had surveyed Jaimec in broad daylight. All the time, Snat lolled in the middle of the cab, gaped glassy-eyed at Mowry's leather case, and responded in monosyllables only when metaphorically beaten over the head.

'This will do,' announced Mowry as they trundled through suburbs and reached a wide crossroad. The truck stopped and he got down. 'Live long!'

'Live long!' responded the driver, and tooled away.

Mowry stood on the sidewalk and thoughtfully watched the truck until it passed from sight. Well, he'd put himself to the first minor test and got by without suspicion. Neither the driver nor Snat had nursed the vaguest idea that he was what they called a Spakum – literally a bedbug – a term for Terrans to which he'd listened with no resentment whatsoever. Nor should James Mowry resent it; until further notice, he was Shir Agavan, a Sirian born and bred.

Holding tight to his case, James Mowry entered the city.

This was Pertane, capital of Jaimec, population a little more than two millions. No other place on the planet approached it in size; it was the centre of Jaimecan civil and military administration, the very heart of the foe's planetary stronghold. By the same token, it was potentially the most dangerous area in which a lone Terran could wander on the loose.

Reaching the downtown section, Mowry tramped around until twilight, considering the location and external appearance of several small hotels. Finally he picked one in a side street off the main stem. Quiet and modest-looking, it would serve for a short time while he sought a better hide-out. But having reached a decision, he did not go straight in.

First, it was necessary to make an up-to-the-minute check of his papers. The documents with which he had been provided were microscopically accurate replicas of those valid within the Sirian Empire nine or ten months ago – but the format might have been changed in the interim. To present papers obviously long out of date was to invite capture on the spot.

He'd better make sure out on the open street where, if it came to the worst, he could throw away his case – along with his bandylegged gait – and run like the devil. So he ambled casually past the hotel and explored nearby streets until he found a policeman. Glancing swiftly around, he marked his getaway route and went up to the officer.

'Pardon, I am a newcomer.' He said it stupidly, putting on a somewhat moronic expression. 'I arrived from Diracta a few days ago.'

'You are lost, *hi?*'

'No, Officer, I am embarrassed.' Mowry fumbled in a pocket, produced his identity card and offered it for inspection. His leg muscles were tensed in readiness for swift and effective flight as he went on. 'A Pertanian friend tells me that my card is wrong because it must now bear a picture of my nude body. This friend is a practical joker, and I do not know whether he is to be believed.'

Frowning, the policeman examined the card's face. He turned it over, studied its back, then returned it. 'This card is quite in order. Your friend is a liar. He would be wise to keep his mouth shut.' The frown grew deeper. 'If he does not, he will someday regret it. The Kaitempi are rough with those who spread false rumours.'

'Yes, Officer,' said Mowry, looking suitably frightened. 'I shall warn him. May you live long!'

'Live long!' said the policeman curtly.

Mowry returned to the hotel, entered as if be owned it, and ordered a room with tub for ten days.

'Your instrument of identity?' asked the clerk.

Mowry passed the card across.

The clerk wrote down its details, handed it back, reversed the register on the counter, and pointed to a line. 'Sign here.'

On taking the room, Mowry's first act was to have a bath. Then he reviewed his position. He had reserved the room for ten days, but that was mere camouflage; he had no intention of staying that long in a place so well surveyed by official eyes. If Sirian habits held good for Jaimec, he could depend upon some snoop examining the hotel register and, perhaps, asking awkward questions before the week was through. He had all the answers ready – but the correct wasp-tactic is not to be asked so long as it can be avoided.

He'd arrived too late in the day to seek and find better sanctuary. Tomorrow would be well-spent finding a rooming house, preferably in a district where the inhabitants tended to mind their own business. Meanwhile, he could put in two or three hours before bedtime studying the lay of the land and estimating future possibilities.

Before starting out, he treated himself to a hearty meal. To a native-born Terran, the food would have seemed strange and somewhat obnoxious; but James Mowry ate with gusto, the flavours serving only to remind him of his childhood. It wasn't until he had finished that he wondered whether some other wasp had ever betrayed himself by being sick at a Sirian table.

For the rest of the evening, his exploration of Pertane was not as haphazard as it looked. He wandered around, memorizing all geographical features that might prove useful to recall later on. But primarily he was seeking to estimate the climate of public opinion with particular reference to minority opinions.

In every war, he knew, no matter how great a government's power its rule is never absolute. In every war, no matter how righteous the cause, the effort is never total. No campaign has ever been fought with the leadership united in favour of it and with the rank and file one hundred per cent behind them.

There is always the minority that opposes a war for such reasons as reluctance to make necessary sacrifices, fear of personal loss or suffering, or philosophical and ethical objection to warfare as a method of settling disputes. Then there is lack of confidence in the ability of the leadership; resentment at being called upon to play a subordinate role; pessimistic belief that victory is far from certain and defeat very possible; egoistic satisfaction of refusing to run with the herd; psychological opposition to being yelled at on any and every petty pretext, and a thousand and one other reasons.

No political or military dictatorship ever has been one hundred per cent successful in identifying and suppressing the malcontents, who bide their time. Mowry could be sure that, by the law of averages, Jaimec must have its share of these. And in addition to the pacifists and quasi-pacifists, there were the criminal classes, whose sole concern in life was to snatch easy money, while avoiding involvement in anything considered unpleasant.

A wasp could make good use of all those who would not hear the bugle call, nor follow the beat of the drum. Indeed, even if it proved impossible to trace any such persons and employ them individually, Mowry could still exploit the fact of their existence.

By midnight, he was back at the hotel confident that Pertane harboured an adequate supply of scapegoats. On buses and in bars he'd had fragmentary conversations with about forty citizens, and had overheard the talk of a hundred more.

Not one had uttered a word definable as unpatriotic, much less treacherous or subversive, but at least a tenth of them had spoken with that vague, elusive air of having more on their minds than they cared to state. In some instances, two of this type conversed together. When that happened it was done with a sort of conspiratorial understanding that any onlooker could recognize fifty yards away, but could never produce as evidence before a military court.

Yes, these – the objectors, the selfish, the greedy, the resentful, the conceited, the moral cowards and the criminals – could all be utilized for Terran purposes.

While lying in bed and waiting for sleep to come, Mowry mentally enrolled the whole of this secret opposition in a mythical organization called *Dirac Angestun Gesept*, the Sirian Freedom Party. He then appointed himself the *DAG's* president, secretary, treasurer, and field-director for the planetary district of Jaimec. The fact that the entire membership was unaware of its status, and had no hand in the election, did not matter.

Neither did it matter that, sooner or later, the Kaitempi would start organizing the collection of members' dues in the form of strangled necks, or that some members might be so lacking in enthusiasm for the cause as to resist payment. If some Sirians could be given the full-time job of hunting down and garroting other Sirians, and if other Sirians could be given the full-time job of dodging or shooting down the garroters, then a distant and different life form would be saved a few unpleasant chores.

With that happy thought, James Mowry – alias Shir Agavan – dozed off. His breathing was suspiciously slow and regular for the purple-faced life form he was supposed to be; his snores were abnormally low-pitched, and he slept flat on his back, instead of lying on his belly. But in the privacy of this room, there were none to hear and see.

THREE

When one man is playing the part of an invading army, the essential thing is to move fast, make full use of any and every opportunity, and waste no effort. James Mowry had to traipse around the city to find a better hide-out. It was equally necessary to go hither and thither to make the first moves in his game; so he combined the two purposes.

He unlocked his bag, opening it carefully with the aid of a special non-conducting plastic key. Despite the fact that he knew exactly what he was doing, a thin trickle of sweat ran down Mowry's spine while he did it. The lock was not so innocent as it looked; in fact, it was a veritable death-trap. He could never quite get rid of the feeling that one of these days it might forget that a plastic key is not a metal lockpick. If ever it did so blunder, the resulting blast area would have a radius of one hundred yards.

Apart from the lethal can wired to the lock, the bag held a dozen small parcels, a mass of printed paper, and nothing else. The paper was of two kinds: stickers and money. There was plenty of the latter; in terms of Sirian guilders, Mowry was a millionaire, and with the additional supply in that distant cave he was a multi-millionaire.

From the bag he took an inch-thick wad of printed stickers – just enough for a day's fast work and, at the same time, few enough to toss away unobserved should the necessity arise. That done, he refastened the bag with the same care.

It was a tricky business, this continual fiddling with a

potential explosion, but it had one great advantage. If any official took it into his head to search the room and check the luggage, the snooper would destroy the evidence along with himself. Moreover, proof of what had happened would be widespread enough to give clear warning to the homecomer.

Departing, he caught a cross-town bus and planted the first sticker on the front window of its upper deck, at a moment when all other seats were vacant. He dismounted at the next stop and casually watched a dozen people boarding the bus. Half of them went upstairs.

The sticker said in bold, easily readable print: *War makes wealth for the few, misery for the many. At the right time, Dirac Angestun Gesept will punish the former, bring aid and comfort to the latter.*

It was sheer luck that he'd arrived coincidentally with a big boost in the war tax; very likely that readers would feel sufficiently aggrieved not to tear the sticker down in a patriotic fury. The chances were equally good that they'd spread the news, and gossip is the same in every part of the mighty cosmos: it gains compound interest as it goes the rounds.

Within five and a half hours he'd disposed of eighty stickers without being caught in the act of affixing them. He'd taken a few risks, had a few narrow squeaks, but never was seen performing the deed. What followed the planting of the fifty-sixth sticker gave him the most satisfaction.

A minor collision on the street resulted in abusive shouts between drivers and drew a mob of onlookers. Taking prompt advantage of the situation, Mowry slapped number fifty-six in the middle of a shop window he found himself backed up against by the crowd, all of whom were looking the other way. He then wormed himself forward and got well into the mob before somebody noticed the window's adornment and attracted general attention to it. The audience turned around, James Mowry with them, and gaped at the discovery.

The finder, a gaunt, middle-aged Sirian with pop eyes, pointed an incredulous finger and stuttered, 'Just l-l-look at that! They must be m-mad in that shop. The Kaitempi will take them all to p-p-prison.'

Mowry edged forward for a better look and read the sticker aloud. *Those who stand upon the platform and openly approve the war will stand upon the scaffold and weepingly regret it. Dirac Angestun Gesept.* He frowned. 'The people in the shop can't be responsible for this – they wouldn't dare.'

'S-somebody's dared,' said Pop Eyes, quite reasonably.

'Yes.' Mowry gave him the hard eye. 'You saw it first. So maybe it was you, *hi?*'

'*Me?*' Pop Eyes went a very pale mauve, that being the nearest a Sirian could get to sheet-white. '*I* didn't put it there. You think I'm c-crazy?'

'Well, as you said, somebody did.'

'It wasn't me,' denied Pop Eyes, angry and agitated. 'It must have been s-some crockpat.'

'Crackpot,' Mowry corrected.

'That's what I just s-said.'

Another Sirian, younger and shrewder, chipped in with, 'That's not a looney's work. There's more to it than that.'

'Why?' demanded Pop Eyes.

'A solitary nut would be more likely to scribble things – silly things, too.' He nodded toward the subject of discussion. 'That's a professional print job. It's also a threat. Somebody risked his neck to plaster it up there. I'll bet there's an illegal organization back of that stunt.'

'It says so, doesn't it?' interjected a voice. 'The Sirian Freedom Party.'

'Never heard of it,' commented another.

'You've heard of it now,' said Mowry.

'S-s-somebody ought to do s-something about it,' declared Pop Eyes waving his arms around.

S-s-somebody did – to wit, a cop. He muscled through the crowd, glowered at the audience and growled, 'Now, what's all this?'

Pop Eyes pointed again, this time with the proprietary air of one who has been granted a patent on the discovery. 'S-see what it s-says on the window.'

The cop looked and saw. Being able to read, he perused it twice while his face went several shades more purple. Then he returned his attention to the crowd. 'Who did this?'

Nobody knew.

'You've got eyes – don't you use them?'

Apparently they didn't.

'Who saw this first?'

'I did,' said Pop Eyes proudly.

'But you didn't see anyone put it up?'

'No.'

The cop stuck out his jaw, 'You sure of that?'

'Yes, Officer,' admitted Pop Eyes, becoming nervous. 'There was an accident in the s-street. We were all watching the two d-d-d—' He got himself into a vocal tangle and choked.

Waving him away, the cop addressed the crowd with considerable menace: 'If anyone knows the identity of the culprit, and refuses to reveal it, he will be deemed equally guilty and will suffer equally when caught.'

Those in front backed off a yard or two; those in the rear suddenly discovered they had business elsewhere. About thirty of the incurably curious stayed put, Mowry among them. He said mildly, 'Maybe they could tell you something in the shop.'

The cop scowled. 'I know my job.'

With that, he gave a loud snort, marched into the shop, and bawled for the manager. In due course that worthy came out, examined his window with horror and swiftly acquired all the symptoms of a nervous wreck.

'We know nothing of this, Officer. I assure you that it is no work of ours. It isn't *inside* the window; it is outside, as you can see. Some passer-by must have done it. I cannot imagine why he should have picked on *this* window. Our patriotic devotion is unquestioned, and . . .'

'Won't take the Kaitempi five seconds to question it,' said the cop cynically.

'But I myself am a reserve officer in the . . .'

'Shut up!' The policeman jerked a heavy thumb toward the offending sticker. 'Get it off.'

'Yes, Officer. Certainly, Officer. I shall remove it immediately.'

The manager started digging with his nails at the sticker's corners, in an attempt to peel it off. He didn't do so well, because Terran technical superiority extended even to common adhesives. After several futile efforts, the manager threw the cop an apologetic look, went inside, came out with a knife, and tried again. This time he succeeded in tearing a small triangle from each corner, leaving the message intact.

'Get hot water and soak it off,' commanded the policeman, rapidly losing patience. He turned and shooed the audience. 'Beat it. Go on, get moving.'

The crowd drew away reluctantly. James Mowry, glancing back from the far corner, saw the manager emerge with a steaming bucket and get busy swabbing the notice. He grinned to himself, knowing that hot water was just the thing to release and activate the hydrofluoric base beneath the print.

Continuing on his way, Mowry disposed of two more stickers where they'd be seen most easily, and cause the most annoyance. It would take twenty minutes for water to free number fifty-six, and at the end of that time he couldn't resist returning to the scene. Going back on his tracks, he ambled past the shop.

Sure enough, the sticker had disappeared; in its place the same message was etched deeply and milkily in the glass. The policeman and the manager were now arguing heatedly upon the sidewalk, with half a dozen citizens gaping alternately at them and the window.

As Mowry walked past, the cop bawled, 'I don't care if the window is valued at two thousand guilders. You've got to board it up or replace the glass.'

'But, Officer . . .'

'Do as you're told. To exhibit subversive propaganda is a major offence, whether intentional or not.'

Mowry wandered away, unnoticed, unsuspected, carrying eighteen stickers still to be used before the day was through. By dusk he'd disposed of them all without mishap. He had also found himself a suitable hideaway.

At the hotel he stopped by the desk and spoke to the clerk. 'This war, it makes things difficult. One can plan nothing with certainty.' He made the hand-splaying gesture that was the Sirian equivalent of a shrug. 'I must leave tomorrow and may be away seven days. It is a great nuisance.'

'You wish to cancel your room, Mr Agavan?'

'No. I reserved it for ten days and will pay for ten.' Dipping into his pocket, Mowry extracted a wad of guilders. 'I shall then be able to claim it if I get back in time. If I don't – well, that'll be my hard luck.'

'As you wish, Mr Agavan.' Indifferent to someone else's throwing good money away, the clerk scribbled a receipt and handed it over.

'Thanks,' said Mowry. 'Live long!'

'May you live long.' The clerk responded in dead tones, obviously not caring if the customer expired on the spot.

James Mowry went to the restaurant and ate; then he returned to his room where he lay full length on the bed, and gave his feet a much-needed rest, while he waited for darkness. When the last streamers of sunset had faded away, he took another pack of stickers from his case, also a piece of crayon, and departed.

The task was much easier this time. Poor illumination helped cover his actions; he was now familiar with the locality and the places most deserving of his attentions; he was not diverted by the need to find another and safer address. For more than four hours he could concentrate upon the job of defacing walls and making a mess of the largest, most expensive sheets of plate glass that would be prominent in daytime.

Between seven-thirty and midnight he slapped exactly one hundred stickers on shops, offices, and vehicles of the city transport system; he also inscribed swiftly, clearly, and in large size the letters *DAG* upon twenty-four walls.

The latter feat was performed with Terran crayon, a deceitfully chalklike substance that made full use of the porosity of brick when water was applied. In other words, the more furiously it was washed the more stubbornly it became embedded.

In the morning he breakfasted, walked out with his case, ignored a line of waiting dynocars, and caught a bus. He changed buses nine times, switching routes one way or the other and heading nowhere in particular. Five times he travelled without his case, which reposed in a rented locker. This may not have been necessary, but there was no way of telling; it was Mowry's duty not only to avoid actual perils but to anticipate hypothetical ones.

Such as this: 'Kaitempi check. Let me see the hotel register. H'm! – much the same as last time. Except for this Shir Agavan. Who is he, *hi!*'

'A forestry surveyor.'

'Did you get that from his identity card?'

'Yes, Officer. It was quite in order.'

'By whom is he employed?'

'By the Ministry of Natural Resources.'

'Was his card embossed with the Ministry's stamp?'

'I don't remember. Maybe it was. I can't say for sure.'

'You should notice things like that. You know full well that you'll be asked about them when the check is made.'

'Sorry, Officer, but I can't see and remember every item that comes my way in a week.'

'You could try harder. Oh, well, I suppose this Agavan character is all right. But maybe I'd better get confirmation, if only to show I'm on the job. Give me your phone.' A call, a few questions, the phone slammed down, then in harsh tones, 'The Ministry has no Shir Agavan upon its roll. The fellow is using a fake identity card. When did he leave the hotel? Did he look agitated when he went? Did he say anything to indicate where he was going? Wake up, you fool, and answer! Give me the key to his room – it must be searched at once. Did he take a dynocar when he departed? Describe him to me as fully as you can. So he was carrying a case? What sort of a case, *hi?*'

That was the kind of chance that must be taken when one holes-up in known and regularly checked haunts. The risk was not enormous – in fact, it was small – but it was still there. And when tried, sentenced, and waiting for death, it is no consolation to know that what came off was a hundred-to-one chance. If Mowry was to maintain the one-man battle, the enemy had to be outwitted all along the line, all the time.

Satisfied that by now the most persistent of snoops could not follow his tortuous trail through the city, Mowry retrieved his case, carried it up to the third floor of a ramshackle tenement building, and let himself into his suite of two sour-smelling rooms. The rest of the day he spent in cleaning the place and making it fit for habitation.

He'd be much harder to trace here. The shifty-eyed landlord had not asked to see his identity card, had accepted him without question as Gast Hurkin, a low-grade railroad official – honest, hard-working, and stupid enough to pay his rent regularly and on time. To the landlord's way of thinking the unsavoury neighbours rated a higher IQ – in terms of their environment – being able to get by with less effort, and remaining tight-mouthed about how they did it.

Housework finished, Mowry bought a paper and searched it for some mention of yesterday's activities. There wasn't a word on the subject. At first he felt disappointed; then, on further reflection, he became heartened.

Opposition to the war and open defiance of the government definitely made news that justified a front-page spread. No reporter, no editor would pass it up if he could help it; therefore the papers had passed it up because they could not help it. Somebody high in authority had clamped down upon them with the heavy hand of censorship. Somebody with considerable power had been driven into making a weak countermove.

That was a start, anyway. Mowry's first waspish buzzings had forced authority to interfere with the press. What's more, the countermove was feeble and ineffective, serving only as a stopgap while officials beat their brains for more decisive measures.

The more persistently a government maintains silence on a given subject of discussion, the more the public talks about it and thinks about it. The longer and more stubborn the silence, the guiltier the government looks to the talkers and thinkers. In time of war, the most morale-lowering question that can be asked is, 'What are they hiding from us *now?*'

Some hundreds of citizens would be asking themselves that same question tomorrow, the next day, or next week. The potent words *Dirac Angestun Gesept* would be on a multitude of lips, milling around in a like number of minds, merely because the powers that be were afraid to talk.

And if a government fears to admit even the pettiest facts of war, how much faith can the common man place in the leadership's claim not to be afraid of anything? *Hi?*

A disease gains in menace when it spreads, popping up in places far apart and taking on the characteristics of an epidemic. For that reason, James Mowry's first outing from his new abode was to Radine, a town forty-two miles south of Pertane: population three hundred thousand, hydroelectric power, bauxite mines, aluminum extraction plants.

He caught an early morning train. It was overcrowded with people compelled to move around by the various needs of war: sullen workers, bored soldiers, self-satisfied officials, colourless nonentities. The seat facing him was occupied by a heavy-bellied character with bloated, porcine features, a caricaturist's idea of the Jaimec Minister of Food.

The train set off, hit up a fast clip. People piled in and out at intermediate stations. Pigface contemptuously ignored Mowry, watched the passing landscape with lordly disdain, finally fell asleep and let his mouth hang open. He was twice as hoglike in his slumbers, and would have attained near-perfection with a lemon in his mouth.

Thirty miles from Radine, the door from the coach ahead slammed open and a civilian policeman entered. He was accompanied by two burly, hard-faced characters in plain clothes. This trio halted by the nearest passenger.

'Your ticket,' demanded the cop.

The passenger handed it over, his expression scared. The policeman examined it front and back, then passed it to his companions, who studied it in turn.

'Your identity card.'

That received the same treatment, the cop looking it over as if doing a routine chore, the other two surveying it more critically and with unconcealed suspicion.

'Your movement permit.'

It passed the triple scrutiny, was given back along with the ticket and identity card. The recipient's face showed vast relief.

The cop picked on the next passenger. 'Your ticket.'

Mowry, seated two-thirds of the way along the coach, observed this performance with much curiosity and a little apprehension. His feelings boosted to alarm when they reached the seventh passenger.

For some reason best known to themselves, the tough-looking pair in plain clothes gazed longer and more intently at this one's documents. Meanwhile, the passenger developed visible signs of agitation. They stared at his strained face, weighing him up. Their own features wore the hungry expressions of predatory animals about to tear down a victim. 'Stand up!' barked one of them.

The passenger shot to his feet and stood quivering. He swayed slightly and it was not due to the rocking of the train. While the cop looked on, the two frisked the passenger. They took things out of his pockets, pawed them around, shoved them back. They patted his clothes all over, showing no respect for his person.

Finding nothing of significance, one of them muttered an oath, then yelled at the victim, 'Well, what's giving you the shakes?'

'I don't feel so good,' said the passenger feebly.

'Is that so? What's the matter with you?'

'Travel sickness. I always get this way in trains.'

'It's a story, anyway.' He glowered at the other, then made a careless gesture. 'All right, you can sit.'

At that the passenger collapsed into his seat and breathed heavily. He had the mottled complexion of one almost sick from fear and relief. The cop eyed him a moment, let go a sniff, then turned his attention to number eight. 'Ticket.'

There were ten more to be chivvied before these inquisitors reached Mowry. He was willing to take a chance on his documents passing muster, but he dared not risk a search. The cop was just a plain, ordinary cop. The other two were members of the all-powerful Kaitempi; if *they* dipped into his pockets, the balloon would go up once and for all. And in due time, when on Terra it was realized that his silence was the silence of the grave, a coldblooded specimen named Wolf would give with the sales talk to another sucker. 'Turn around. Walk bowlegged. We want you to become a wasp.'

By now, most of the passengers were directing their full attention along the aisle, watching what was going on and meanwhile trying to ooze an aura of patriotic rectitude. James Mowry slid a surreptitious look at Pigface. Were those sunken little eyes really closed, or were they watching him between narrowed lids?

Short of pushing his face right up against the other's unpleasant countenance, he couldn't tell for certain. But it made no difference; the trio were edging nearer every moment, and he had to take a risk. Furtively he felt behind him, found a tight but deep gap in the upholstery where the bottom of the back rest met the rear of the seat. Keeping his attention riveted upon

Pigface, he edged a pack of stickers and two crayons out of his pocket, crammed them into the gap, poking them well out of sight. The sleeper opposite did not stir or blink an eyelid.

Two minutes later, the cop gave Pigface an irritable shove on the shoulder and that worthy woke up with a snort. He glared at the cop, then at the pair in plain clothes. 'So! What is this?'

'Your ticket,' said the cop.

'A traffic check, *hi?*' responded Pigface, showing sudden understanding. 'Oh, well . . .' Inserting fat fingers in a vest pocket, he took out an ornate card embedded in a slice of transparent plastic. This he exhibited to the trio, and the cop stared and became servile; the two toughies stiffened like raw recruits caught dozing on parade.

'Your pardon, Major,' apologized the cop.

'It is granted,' assured Pigface, showing a well-practised mixture of arrogance and condescension. 'You are only doing your duty.' He favoured the rest of the coach with a beam of triumph, openly enjoying the situation and advertising himself as being several grades above the common herd.

Embarrassed, the cop switched to Mowry, and said, 'Ticket.'

Mowry handed it over, striving to look innocent and bored. Pseudo-nonchalance didn't come easy because now he was the focal point of the coach's battery of eyes. Almost all the other passengers were looking his way; Major Pigface was surveying him speculatively, and the two Kaitempi agents were giving him the granite-hard stare.

'Identity card.'

That got passed across.

'Movement permit.'

He surrendered it and braced himself for the half-expected command of, 'Stand up!'

It did not come. Anxious to get away from the major's cold, official gaze, the three examined the papers, handed them back without comment, and moved on. Mowry shoved the documents into his pocket, tried to keep a great relief out of his voice as he spoke to the other: 'I wonder what they're after.'

'It is no business of yours,' said Major Pigface, as insultingly as possible.

'No, of course not,' agreed Mowry.

There was silence between them. The major gazed out the window and showed no inclination to resume his slumbers. *Damn the fellow*, thought Mowry; retrieving the stickers was going to prove difficult with that slob awake and alert.

A door crashed shut as the cop and Kaitempi agents finished with that coach and went through to the following one. A minute later, the train pulled up with such suddenness that a couple of passengers were thrown from their seats. Outside the train, and farther back toward the rear end, voices started shouting.

Heaving himself to his feet, Major Pigface opened the window's top half, stuck his head out and looked back toward the source of the noise. Then, with a speed surprising in one so cumbersome, he whipped a gun from his pocket, ran along the aisle and through the end door. Outside, the bawling grew louder.

Mowry got up and had a look through the window. Near the tail of the train a small bunch of figures were running alongside the track, the cop and the Kaitempi slightly in the lead. As he watched, the latter swung up their right arms; several sharp cracks rang through the morning air. It was impossible to see at whom they were shooting.

Also beside the train, gun in hand, the major was pounding heavily along in pursuit of the pursuers. Curious faces popped out of windows all along the line of coaches.

Mowry called to the nearest face, 'What happened?'

'Those three came in to check papers. Some fellow saw them, made a wild dash to the opposite door and jumped out. They stopped the train and went after him. He got a pretty good start. They'll be lucky to catch him.'

'Who was he, anyway?'

'No idea. Some wanted criminal, I suppose.'

'Well,' offered Mowry, 'if the Kaitempi come after me, I'd hotfoot it like a scared Spakum.'

'Who wouldn't?' said the other.

Withdrawing, James Mowry took his seat. All the other travellers were at the windows, their full attention directed outside. This was an opportune moment. He dug a hand into the hiding-place, extracted the stickers and crayons, pocketed them.

The train stayed put for half an hour, during which there was no more excitement within hearing. Finally it jerked into motion and at the same time Major Pigface reappeared and dumped himself into his seat. He looked sour enough to pickle his own hams.

'Did you catch him?' asked Mowry, lending his manner all the politeness and respect he could muster.

The major bestowed a dirty look on him. 'It is no business of yours.'

'No, of course not.'

The previous silence came back and remained until the train pulled into Radine. This being the terminus, everybody got out. Mowry padded along with the mob through the station exit, but did not make a beeline for windows and walls on which to affix his messages.

Instead, he followed the major.

FOUR

Shadowing presented no great difficulty. Major Pigface behaved as if the possibility of his being trailed would be the last thing ever to enter his mind. He went his way with the arrogant assurance of one who has the law in his pocket, all ordinary persons being less than the dust.

Immediately outside the station's arched entrance, the major turned right and plodded a hundred yards along the approach-road to the car-park at the farther end. Here he stopped by a long green dynocar and felt in his pocket for keys.

Lingering in the shadow of a projecting buttress, James Mowry watched his quarry unlock the door and squeeze inside. He hustled across the road to a taxi-stand, climbed into the leading vehicle. The move was perfectly timed; he sank into the seat just as the green dynocar whined past.

'Where to?' asked the taxi driver.

'Can't tell you exactly,' said Mowry, evasively. 'I've been here only once before and that was years ago. But I know the way. Just follow my instructions.'

The taxi's dynamo set up a rising hum as the machine sped down the road, while its passenger kept attention on the car ahead and gave curt orders from time to time. It would have been lots easier, he knew, to have pointed and said, 'Follow that green car.' But that would have linked him in the driver's mind with the major, or at least with the major's green dyno. The Kaitempi were experts at ferreting out such links and following them to the bitter end. As it was, the taxi driver had no idea that he was shadowing anyone.

Swiftly the chaser and the chased threaded their way through the centre of Radine, until eventually the leader made a sharp turn to the left and rolled down a ramp into the basement of a large apartment building. Mowry let the taxi run a couple of hundred yards farther on before he called a halt.

'This will do me.' He got out, felt for money. 'Nice to have a good, dependable memory, isn't it?'

'Yar,' said the driver. 'One guilder six-tenths.'

Mowry gave him two guilders and watched him cruise away. Hastening back to the apartment building, he entered, took an inconspicuous seat in its huge foyer, leaned back, and pretended to be enjoying a semi-doze while waiting for someone. There were several others sitting around, but none took notice of him.

Sure enough, he hadn't been there half a minute when Major Pigface came into the other end of the foyer from a door leading to the basement garage. Without so much as a glance around, the major stepped into one of a bank of small automatic elevators. The door slid shut. The illuminated telltale on the lintel winked off numbers, stopped at seven, held it awhile, then returned downward to zero. The door glided open, showing the box now empty.

After another five minutes, Mowry yawned, stretched, consulted his watch and went out. He paced along the street until he found a phone booth. From it, he called the apartment building, got its switchboard operator.

'I was supposed to meet somebody in your foyer nearly an hour ago,' he explained. 'I can't make it. If he's still waiting, I'd like him to be told I've been detained.'

'Who is he?' asked the operator. 'A resident?'

'Yes – but I've clean forgotten his name. Nobody is more stupid than me about names. He's plump, has heavy features, lives on the seventh floor. Major . . . Major . . . what a *soko* of a memory I've got!'

'That would be Major Sallana,' the operator said.

'Correct,' agreed Mowry, 'Major Sallana – I had it at the back of my mind all the time.'

'Hold on. I'll see if he's still waiting.' There followed a minute's silence before the operator returned with, 'No, he isn't. I've just called his apartment and there's no reply. Do you wish to leave a message for him?'

'It won't be necessary – he must have given me up. It's not of great importance, anyway. Live long!'

'Live long!' said the operator.

So there was no reply from the apartment; it looked as if Major Sallana had gone straight in and straight out again – unless he was in his bath. That didn't seem likely; he'd hardly had time to fill a tub, undress and get into it. If he really was absent from his rooms, opportunity had presented itself so far as Mowry was concerned; it was up to him to grab it while it was there.

Despite an inward sense of urgency, Mowry paused long enough to cope with other work. He looked through the booth's glass, found himself unobserved, then slapped a sticker on the facing window exactly where tireless talkers could contemplate it while holding the phone.

It said: *Power-lovers started this war. Dirac Angestun Gesept will end it – and them!*

Returning to the apartments, he strolled with deceitful confidence across the foyer and stepped into an unoccupied elevator. He turned to face the open front, became conscious of someone hurrying toward the bank, glanced that way and was aghast to see the major approaching.

The fellow was wearing a ruminative scowl; he hadn't yet seen Mowry, but undoubtedly would do so unless the wasp moved fast. Mowry slammed the door and prodded the third button on the panel. The elevator glided up to the third floor, stopped. He kept it there, the door still shut, until he heard the whine of an adjoining box passing him and going higher. Then he dropped back to ground level and left the building. He felt

41

thwarted and short-tempered, and cursed his luck in a steady undertone.

Between then and mid-evening he worked off his ire by decorating Radine with one hundred and twenty stickers and fourteen chalked walls. Then, deciding to call it a day for that kind of work, he dropped the remaining half-stick of crayon down a grid.

At the ten-time hour, he chomped through an overdue meal, having eaten nothing since breakfast. That finished, he looked up Sallana's number, called it, got no reply. *Now* was the time. Repeating his earlier tactic, he went to the building, took an elevator to the seventh floor, this time without mishap. He trod silently along the heavy carpet of the corridor, looking at doors until he found one bearing the name he sought.

He knocked.

No answer.

He knocked again, a little louder but not loud enough to arouse others nearby.

Silence answered him.

This was where James Mowry's hectic schooling paid off. Taking from his pocket a bunch of keys that looked quite ordinary but weren't, he set to work on the lock and had the door open within precisely thirty-five seconds. Speed was essential for the task – if anyone had chosen that time to enter the corridor, Mowry would have been caught red-handed.

He slipped through the door, carefully closed it behind him. His first act was to make swift survey of the rooms and assure himself that nobody was lying around, asleep or drunk. There were four rooms, all vacant. Definitely Major (Pigface) Sallana was not at home.

Returning to the first room, Mowry gave it a careful once-over and spotted a gun lying atop a small filing cabinet. He checked it, found it loaded and stuck it in his pocket.

Next, he cracked open a big, heavy desk and started raking through its drawers. The way he did it had the sure superfast touch of the professional criminal, but was in fact a tribute to his college training.

The contents of the fourth drawer on the left made his hair stand on end. He had been searching with the intention of confiscating whatever it was that made cops servile, and even persuaded Kaitempi agents to stand to attention. Jerking open the drawer, Mowry found himself gazing at a neat stack of writing paper bearing official print across its head.

This was more than he'd expected, more than he had hoped for in his most optimistic moments. To his mind it proved that, despite his college lectures about caution, caution, everlasting, unremitting caution, it pays to play hunches and take chances. What the paper's caption said was:

DIRAC KAIMINA TEMPITI.
Leshun Radine.

In other words: the Sirian Secret Police – District of Radine. No wonder those toughs on the train had been quick to grovel: the major was a Kaitempi brass hat and as such outranked an army brigadier, or even a space-navy fleet leader.

This discovery upped the speed of Mowry's activity still further. From the pile of luggage in the back room he seized a small case, forced it open and tossed the clothing it contained onto the floor. He dumped all the Kaitempi writing paper into the case. A little later he found a small embossing machine, tested it and found that it impressed the letters *DKT* surmounted by a winged sword. That also went into the case.

Finishing with the desk, he started on the adjacent filing cabinet, his nostrils twitching with excitement as he worked at its top drawer. A faint sound came to his ears; he stopped, taut and listening. It was the scrape of a key in the door lock. The key failed to turn at the first attempt.

Mowry jumped toward the wall, flattened himself against it where he'd be concealed by the opening door. The key grated a second time, the lock responded, the door swung across his field of vision as Sallana lumbered in.

The major took four paces into the room before his brain accepted what his eyes could see. He came to a full stop, stared incredulously and with mounting fury at the ransacked desk while behind him the door drifted around and clicked shut. Reaching a decision, he turned to go out and then saw the invader.

'Good evening,' greeted Mowry, flat-voiced.

'*You?*' The major glowered at him with outraged authority. 'What are you doing here? What is the meaning of this?'

'I'm here as a common thief. The meaning is that you've been robbed.'

'Then let me tell you—'

'When robbery is done,' Mowry went on, 'somebody has to be the victim. This time it's your turn. No reason why you should have all the luck all the time, is there?'

Major Sallana took a step forward.

'Sit down!' ordered Mowry.

The other stopped but did not sit. He stood firm upon the carpet, his small, crafty eyes taking on a stubborn glint. 'Put down that gun.'

'Who? – Me?' asked Mowry.

'You don't know what you're doing,' declared Sallana, conditioned by a lifetime of creating fear. 'Because you don't know who I am. But when you do, you'll wish . . .'

'As it happens, I do know who you are,' Mowry chipped in. 'You're one of the Kaitempi's fat rats. A professional torturer, a paid strangler, a conscienceless *soko* who maims and kills for money, and for the pleasure of it. Now sit down when I tell you.'

Still, the major refused to sit. On the contrary, he refuted the popular belief that all bullies are cowards; like many of his ilk, he had brute courage. He took a heavy but swift step to one side while his hand dived into a pocket.

But the eyes that so often had calmly watched the death

throes of others had now betrayed him to his own end. The step had hardly been taken, the hand only just reached the pocket, when James Mowry's gun went *br-r-r-up!*, not loudly but effectively. For five or six seconds Major Sallana stood wearing a stupid expression; then he teetered, fell backward with a thud that shook the room, rolled onto his side. His thick legs gave a couple of spasmodic jerks, then went still.

Gently opening the door a few inches, Mowry gazed into the corridor. There came no rush of feet toward the apartment; nobody raced away yelling for help. If anyone had heard the muffled burst of shots, they must have attributed the noise to the flow of traffic far below.

Satisfied that the alarm had not been raised, he shut the door, bent over the body and had a close look at it. Sallana was as dead as he could be, the brief spray from the machine pistol having put seven slugs through his obese frame.

It was a pity, in a way, because Mowry would have liked to hammer, kick, or otherwise get out of him the answers to some cogent questions. There were many other things he wanted to know about the Kaitempi – in particular the identities of its current victims, their physical condition and where they were hidden. No wasp could find supporters more loyal and enthusiastic than genuine natives of the planet rescued from the strangler's noose.

But one cannot force information from a corpse. That was his sole regret. In all other respects, he had cause for gratification. For one thing, factual evidence of the methods of the Kaitempi was of such a revolting nature that to remove any one of them was to do a favour to Sirians and Terrans alike. For another, such a killing was an ideal touch in present circumstances; it lent murderous support to stickers and wall-scrawls.

It was a broad hint to the powers that be that somebody was willing and able to do more than talk. The wasp had done plenty of buzzing around; now it had demonstrated its sting.

He frisked the body and got what he had coveted from the

moment Sallana had basked in adulation upon the train: the ornate card set in thin plastic. It bore signs, seals and signatures, certified that the bearer held the rank of major in the Secret Police. Better still, it did not give the bearer's name and personal description, contenting itself with using a code number. The Secret Police were secret even among themselves, a habit of which others could take full advantage.

Mowry now returned his attention to the filing cabinet. Most of the material within it proved to be worthless, revealing nothing not already known to Terran Intelligence. But there were three files containing case histories of persons made to conform to the Kaitempi habit of hiding identities under code numbers. Evidently the major had abstracted them from local headquarters and taken them home to study at leisure.

Mowry scanned these papers rapidly. It soon became clear that the three unknowns were potential rivals to those already in power. The case histories said nothing to indicate whether their subjects were now living or dead. The implication was that their fate had yet to be decided; otherwise it seemed hardly likely that Sallana would waste time on such documents. Anyway, the disappearance of these vital papers would irritate the powers that be, and possibly frighten a few of them.

So Mowry put the files in the case along with the rest of the loot. After that, he made a swift hunt around for anything previously overlooked, searched spare suits in the bedroom, but discovered nothing more worth taking. The last chore was to remove all clues capable of linking him with the existing situation.

With the case in one hand, and the gun in his pocket, Mowry paused in the doorway and looked back at the body. 'Live long!'

Major (Pigface) Sallana did not deign to reply. He reposed in silence, his pudgy right hand clasping a paper on which was inscribed: *Executed by Dirac Angestun Gesept.*

Whoever found the body would be sure to pass that message on. It would be equally certain to go from hand to hand, up the ascending scale of rank, right to the top brackets. With any luck at all, it would give a few of them the galloping jitters.

Luck held; James Mowry did not have to wait long for a train to Pertane. He was more than glad of this, because the bored station police tended to become inquisitive about travellers who sat around too long. True, if accosted he could show his documents or – strictly as a last resort – use the stolen Kaitempi card to browbeat his way out of a possible trap. But it was better and safer not to become an object of attention in this place at this time.

The train came in and he managed to get aboard without having been noticed by any of several cops. After a short time it pulled out again and rumbled into pitch-darkness. The lateness of the hour meant that passengers were few, and the coach he had chosen had plenty of vacant seats. It was easy to select a place where he would not be pestered by a garrulous neighbour, or studied for the full length of the journey by someone with sharp eyes and a long memory.

One thing was certain: if Sallana's body were found within the next three or four hours, the resulting hullabaloo would spread fast enough and far enough to ensure an end-to-end search of the train. The searchers would have no subject's description to go upon, but they'd take a look into all luggage, and recognize stolen property when they found it.

Mowry dozed uneasily to the hypnotic thrum-tiddy-thrum of the train. Every time a door slammed or a window rattled he awoke, nerves stretched, body tense. A couple of times he wondered whether a top priority radio-call was beating the train to its destination.

'Halt and search all passengers and luggage on the eleven-twenty from Radine.'

There was no check on the way. The train slowed, clanked through the points and switches of a large grid system, and rolled into Pertane. Its passengers dismounted, all of them sleepy, and a few looking half-dead, as they straggled untidily toward the exit. Mowry timed himself to be in the rear of the bunch, lagging behind with half a dozen bandy-legged moochers. His full attention was directed straight ahead, watching for evidence of a grim-faced bunch waiting at the barrier.

If they were really there, in ambush for him, there'd be only two courses open to him. He could drop the case and with it the valuable loot, shoot first and fastest, make a bolt, and hope to get away in the ensuing confusion. As a tactic, it would give him the advantage of surprise. But failure meant immediate death, and even success might be dearly bought with a couple of bullets in the body.

Alternatively, he could try bluff by marching straight up to the biggest and ugliest of them, shoving the case into his hands and saying with dopey eagerness, 'Pardon, Officer, but one of those fellows who just went through dropped this in front of me. I can't imagine why he abandoned his luggage.' Then, somewhere in the resulting chaos, there should be a chance for him to amble around a corner and run as if jet-propelled.

He was sweaty with reaction when he found his fears were not confirmed. This had been his first murder, and it *was* a murder because they would define it as such. So he'd been paying for it in his own imagination, fancying himself hunted before the hunt was on. Beyond the barrier lounged two station police, eyeing the emerging stream with total lack of interest and yawning from time to time. He went past practically under their noses, and they could not have cared less about him.

But James Mowry wasn't off the hook yet. Police at the station expected to see people carrying luggage any time of the day or night. Cops in the city streets were inclined to question the reason at such an hour.

That problem could be solved by the easy expedient of taking a taxi – only to create another problem. Taxis have to be driven, and the most taciturn of them could become posit- ively gabby when questioned by the Kaitempi.

'You take anyone off the eleven-twenty from Radine?'

'Yar. Young fellow with a case.'

'Notice anything suspicious about him? He act tough or behave warily, for instance?'

'Not that I noticed. Seemed all right to me. Wasn't a native Jaimecan, though. Spoke with a real Mashambi growl.'

'Remember where you took him, *hi?*'

'Yar, I do. I can show you.'

There was a way out of this predicament; Mowry took it by putting the case in a rented locker in the station and walking away. In theory, the case should be safe enough for one full Jaimecan day; in fact, there was a chance of its being discovered and used as bait.

On a world where nothing was sacrosanct, the Kaitempi had master keys to almost everything. They weren't above opening and searching every bank of lockers within a thousand miles of the scene of the crime, if they took it into their heads that to do so would be a smart move. So when he returned in daytime to collect the case, Mowry would have to approach the lockers with considerable caution, making sure that a watch was not being kept upon them by a ring of hard characters.

Pacing rapidly home, he was within half a mile of his destination when two cops stepped from a dark doorway on the other side of the street. 'Hey, you!'

Mowry stopped. They came across, stared at him in grim silence. Then one made a gesture to indicate the high-shining stars, the deserted street. 'Wandering around pretty late, aren't you?'

'Nothing wrong with that, is there?' he answered, making his tone slightly apologetic.

'*We* are asking the questions,' retorted the cop. 'Where've you been to this hour?'

'On a train.'

'From where?'

'Khamasta.'

'And where're you going now?'

'Home.'

'You'd have made it quicker in a taxi, wouldn't you?'

49

'Sure would,' Mowry agreed. 'Unfortunately I happened to be the last out. Someone always has to be last out. By that time every taxi had been grabbed.'

'Well, it's a story.'

At this point, the other cop adopted Technique Number Seven – namely, a narrowing of the eyes, an out-thrusting of the jaw, and a harshening of the voice. Once in a while Number Seven would be rewarded with a guilty look, or a hopelessly exaggerated expression of innocence. He was very good at it, having practised it assiduously upon his wife and the bedroom mirror.

'You wouldn't perhaps have been nowhere near Khamasta, *hi?* You wouldn't perhaps have been spending the night taking a nice, easy stroll around Pertane and sort of absent-mindedly messing around with walls and windows, would you?'

'No, I wouldn't,' said Mowry, 'because nobody would pay me a bad guilder for my trouble. Do I look crazy?'

'Not enough to be noticed,' admitted the cop. 'But somebody's doing it, crazy or not.'

'Well, I can't blame you fellows for wanting to nab him. I don't like loonies myself. They give me the creeps.' He made an impatient gesture. 'If you're going to search me, how about getting the job done? I've had a long day, I'm dog-tired and I want to get home.'

'I don't think we'll bother,' said the cop. 'You show us your identity card.'

Mowry dug it out. The cop gave it no more than a perfunctory glance, while his companion ignored it altogether.

'All right, on your way. If you insist on walking the streets at this hour, you must expect to be stopped and questioned. There's a war on, see?'

'Yes, Officer,' said Mowry meekly.

He pushed off at his best pace, thanking heaven he had got rid of his luggage. If he'd been holding that case, they'd have regarded it, rightly enough, as probable evidence of evil-doing. To prevent them from opening it and inspecting the contents, he'd have had to subdue them with the Kaitempi card. He didn't want to make use of that tactic, if he could help it, until sometime after Sallana's killing had been discovered and the resulting uproar had died down. Say in at least one month's time.

Reaching his apartment, James Mowry undressed but did not go immediately to sleep. He lay in bed and examined the precious card again and again. Now that he had more time to ponder its full significance and obvious potentialities, he found himself torn two ways – should he keep it or not?

The socio-political system of the Sirian Empire being what it was, a Kaitempi card was the prime scare-device on any Sirian-held planet. The mere sight of this dreaded totem was enough to make ninety-nine per cent of the civilians get down on their knees and salaam. That fact made a Kaitempi card of tremendous value to any wasp. Yet Terra had not provided him with such a weapon; he'd had to grab it for himself. The obvious conclusion was that Terran Intelligence lacked an original copy.

Out there amid the mist of stars, on the green-blue world called Earth, they could duplicate anything save a living entity – and could produce a close imitation even of that. Maybe they needed this card. Given the chance, maybe they'd arm every wasp with a mock-majorship in the Kaitempi.

For Mowry himself, to surrender the card would be like voluntarily sacrificing his queen while playing a hard-fought and bitter game of chess. All the same, before going to sleep he reached his conclusion: on his first return to the cave he would beam a detailed report of what had happened, the prize he had won and what it was worth. Terra could then decide whether or not to deprive him of it in the interest of the greater number.

FIVE

At noon, Mowry returned to the station cautiously, and stood around for twenty minutes, as if waiting to meet an incoming traveller. He kept careful watch in all directions while appearing interested in nothing save occasional streams of arrivals. Some fifty or sixty other people were idling about in unconscious imitation of himself; among them, he could detect nobody maintaining a sly eye upon the lockers. There were about a dozen who looked overmuscled, and wore the deadpan hardness of officials; but these were solely interested in people coming through the barriers.

Finally he took the chance; he ambled casually up to his locker, stuck his key in its door, wishing that he had a third eye located in the back of his neck. Opening the door, he took out the case and had a bad moment as he stood with the damning evidence in his hand. If ever it was going to occur, now was the time for a shout of triumph, a sudden grip on his shoulder and a bunch of callous faces all around.

Still, nothing happened. James Mowry strolled away looking blandly innocent, but deep inside as leery as a fox who hears the dim, distant baying of the hounds. Outside the station, he jumped a crosstown bus and maintained a wary watch for followers. The chances were very high that nobody had noticed him.

Perhaps nobody was interested in him, because in Radine the Kaitempi were still running around in circles, without the vaguest notion of where to probe first. But Mowry could not take that for granted, nor dare he underestimate the enemy's craftiness. There was one chance in a thousand that, by some item he'd overlooked, he'd given them a lead straight to the lockers. It might be that they had decided not to nab him on the spot, hoping that he'd take them to the rest of the presumed mob. The Kaitempi were not the kind to alarm a gang by grabbing one member; they preferred to bide their time and take the lot.

So during the ride he peered repeatedly backward, observed passengers getting on and off, and tried to see if he could spot a loaded dynocar tagging along somewhere behind. He changed buses five times, detoured through two squalid alleys, and walked into the fronts and out the backs of three department stores.

Satisfied at last that there was no surreptitious pursuit, he made for his apartment, kicked the case under the bed and let go a deep sigh. Mowry had been warned that this kind of life would prove a continual strain on the nerves. It was!

Going out again, he bought a box of envelopes and a cheap typewriter. Then, using the Kaitempi paper, he spent the rest of the day and part of the next one typing with forceful brevity. He didn't have to bother about leaving his prints all over this correspondence; Terran fingerprint treatment had turned his impressions into vague, unclassifiable blotches.

When he had finished that task, he devoted the following day to patient research in the city library. He made copious notes, went home, then addressed and stamped a stack of envelopes.

In the early evening, he mailed more than two hundred letters to newspaper editors, radio announcers, military leaders, senior civil servants, police chiefs, prominent politicians and key members of the government. Typed under the Kaitempi heading and supported by the embossed seal of its winged sword, the message was short:

Sallana is the first.
There are plenty more to come.
The list is long.
Dirac Angestun Gesept.

That done, he burned the envelope box and dropped the typewriter in the river where it ran deep. If Mowry had occasion to write any more letters, he'd buy another typewriter and then get rid of it the same way. He could well afford to buy and scrap a hundred typewriters if he thought it necessary. The more the merrier. If the Kaitempi analyzed the type on threatening correspondence and found a number of untraceable machines being used, they'd get the idea that a gigantic organization was at work. Furthermore, his every purchase helped inflate the Jaimecan economy with worthless paper.

His next step was to visit a drive-yourself agency and rent a dynocar for a week, using the name of Shir Agavan and the address of the hotel where first he'd holed-up. By its means he got rid of five hundred stickers distributed over six small towns and thirty villages. The job was a lot riskier than it had been in Radine or Pertane.

The villages were by far the worst to handle; the smaller in size, the more troublesome they proved. In a city of a quarter million to two million population, a stranger is an insignificant nonentity; in a hamlet of less than one thousand inhabitants he is noticed, remarked upon, and his every move watched.

On many occasions a bunch of yokels gave him the chance to slap up a sticker by switching attention from him to his car. Twice somebody took down the car's number just for the fun of it. It was a good thing he'd given a blind-alley lead when hiring the car, because police inquiries about the widespread rash of subversive stickers would almost certainly make them relate the phenomenon to the laconic, fast-moving stranger driving dyno XC17978.

*

James Mowry had been on Jaimec exactly four weeks when he disposed of the last of the stickers from his bag, and thus reached the end of phase one. It was at this point he began to feel despondent.

In the papers, and over the air, officialdom still maintained complete silence about traitorous activities. Not a word had been said about the slaughter of Major Sallana. All the outward evidence suggested that the government remained unaware of waspish buzzings, and was totally unconcerned about the existence of an imaginary *Dirac Angestun Gesept.*

Thus deprived of visible reactions, Mowry had no way of telling what results he had achieved, if any. In retrospect this paper war looked pretty futile, in spite of all Wolf's glib talk about pinning down an army with little more than gestures. He, Mowry, had been lashing out in the dark and the other fellow wasn't even bothering to hit back.

That made it difficult to maintain enthusiasm at the first feverish pitch. Just one public squeal of pain from the opposition – or a howl of fury, or a tirade of threats – would have given Mowry's morale a boost by showing him that at last he had landed a wallop on something solid. But they hadn't given him the petty satisfaction of hearing them breathing hard.

He was paying the psychological penalty of working alone. There was no companion-in-arms with whom to share stimulating speculations about the enemy's hidden counter-moves; nobody to encourage, or from whom to receive encouragement; nobody sharing the conspiracy, the danger, and – as is usual among two or more – the laughs.

He built up a blue spell so depressing that for two days he stayed around the apartment and did nothing but mope. On the third day, pessimism was replaced with a sense of alarm. He did not ignore the new feeling; at training college they'd warned him times without number always to heed it.

'The fact that one is hunted in deadly earnest can cause an abnormal sharpening of the mental perceptions, almost to the point of developing a sixth sense. That's what makes hardened criminals difficult to catch. They get hunches and play them. Many a badly wanted crook has moved out one jump ahead of the police with such timeliness that they've suspected a tip-off. All that had really happened was that the fellow suddenly got the jitters and took off good and fast. For the sake of your skin, you do the same. If ever you feel they're getting close, don't hang around and try to check on it – just beat it somewhere else!'

Yes, that's what they'd said. He remembered wondering whether this ability to smell danger might be quasi-telepathic. The police rarely pulled a raid without a stakeout, or some sort of preliminary observation. A hound hanging around a hole – sharp-eyed, sharp-toothed, and unable to avoid thinking of what he was doing – might give the one in hiding his mental scent. It would register not in clear thought-forms but rather as the inward shrilling of an alarm bell.

On the strength of that, Mowry grabbed his bags and bolted out the back way. Nobody was loafing around at that moment; nobody saw him go; nobody tracked him as he went.

Four beefy characters stationed themselves within watching and shooting distance of the back a little before midnight. Two carloads of similar specimens drew up at the front, bashed open the door, charged upstairs. They were there three hours, and they half-killed the landlord before they became convinced of his ignorance.

Mowry knew nothing of this; it was the much-needed boost that he was lucky to miss.

His new sanctuary, a mile and a half distant, was one long, narrow room at the top of a dilapidated building in Pertane's toughest quarter – a district where the technique of house-keeping was to kick the dirt around until it got lost. Here he had not been asked for any name or identity card, it being one of the more delightful customs of the locality to mind one's own business. All that proved necessary was to exhibit a fifty-guilder note. The money had been snatched, a cheap and well-worn key given in exchange.

Promptly he made the key useless by buying a cruciform multiward lock and fitting it to the door. He also fixed a couple of recessed bolts to the window, despite the fact that it was forty feet above ground and well-nigh unreachable. Finally he built a small hidden trap in the roof, an escape route if ever the stairs became solidly blocked with enemy carcasses.

For the time being, James Mowry decided, his chief danger lay in the neighbouring small-time thieves – the big ones wouldn't bother to cut their way into a single room in a slum. The locks and bolts should suffice to keep out the pikers.

Again he had to spend some time in making the place fit for Terran habitation. If ever he was caught by the Kaitempi, he'd roll in the deep, stinking filth of a deathcell; but so long as he remained free, Mowry insisted on his right to be fastidious. By the time he'd finished his housework, the room was brighter and sweeter than it had been since the builders moved out and the proletariat moved in.

By now he'd recovered from both his depression and his sense of impending disaster. In better spirits he went out-doors and walked along the road until he reached a vacant lot littered with junk. When nobody was looking he dropped Major Sallana's gun there, near the sidewalk where it could easily be seen.

Ambling onward with hands in pockets, his gait a bowlegged slouch, he reached a doorway, lounged in it and assumed the look of bored cunning worn by one who sows nor neither doth he reap. This was the fashionable expression in that area. Mostly his gaze was aimed across the street, but he was keeping surreptitious watch upon the gun lying seventy yards away.

What followed proved yet again that not one person in ten uses his eyes. Within a short time, thirty people had passed close by the gun without seeing it. Six of these walked within a few inches of it; one actually stepped over it.

Finally someone spotted it. He was a shrivel-chested spindle-legged youth with splotches of darker purple on his face. Halting by the gun, he stared at it, bent over for a closer look but did not touch it. Then he glanced hurriedly around, but failed to see the watching Mowry, who had retreated farther into the doorway. Again he bent toward the gun, put out a hand as if to grab it. At the last moment he changed his mind and hastened away.

'Wanted it but too scared to take it,' Mowry decided.

Twenty more pedestrians passed. Of these, two noticed the gun and pretended they hadn't seen it. Neither came back to claim it when nobody was near; probably they viewed the weapon as dangerous evidence that someone had seen fit to dump – and they weren't going to be caught with it. The one who eventually confiscated it was an artist in his own right.

This character, a heavily built individual with hanging jowls and a rolling gait, went by the gun. Continuing onward, he stopped at the next corner – fifty yards away – and looked around with the air of a stranger uncertain of his whereabouts. Then he took a notebook from his pocket and put on a great play of consulting it. All the time, his sharp little eyes were darting this way and that; but they failed to find the watcher in the doorway.

After a while, he retraced his steps, crossed the vacant lot, dropped the notebook on top of the gun, scooped up both in one swift snatch, and ambled casually onward. The way the book remained prominently in his hand while the gun disappeared was a wonder to behold.

Letting the fellow get a good lead, Mowry emerged from the doorway and followed. He hoped the other had only a short way to go. This, obviously, was a smart customer likely to notice and throw off a shadower. Mowry didn't want to lose him after the trouble he'd taken to find a willing gun-grabber.

Floppy Jowls continued along the road, turned right into a narrower and dirtier street, then headed over a crossroad, turned left. At no time did he behave suspiciously, take evasive tactics, or show any awareness of being followed.

Near the end of the street he entered a cheap hashery with dusty windows and a cracked, unreadable sign above its door. A few moments later, James Mowry strolled past and gave the place a swift once-over. It looked like a typical rathole where underworld characters waited for the night. But nothing ventured, nothing gained; he shoved open the door and walked in.

The place stank of unwashed bodies, stale food and drippings of *zith*. Behind the bar, a sallow-faced attendant eyed him with the hostile expression reserved for any and every unfamiliar face. A dozen customers, sitting in the half-light by the stained and paintless wall, glowered at him on general principles. They looked like a choice collection of hoods.

Mowry leaned on the bar and spoke to Sallow Face, making his tones sound tough. 'I'll have a mug of coffee.'

'*Coffee?*' The other jumped as if rammed with a needle. 'Blood of Jaime, that's a *Spakum* drink.'

'Yar,' said Mowry. 'I want to spit it all over the floor.' He laughed harshly. 'Wake up and give me a *zith*.'

The attendant scowled, snatched a none-too-clean glassite mug from a shelf, pumped it full of low-grade *zith* and slid it across. 'Six-tenths.'

Paying him, Mowry took the drink across to a small table in the darkest corner, a dozen pairs of eyes following his every move. He sat down, looked idly around, his manner that of one thoroughly at home when slumming. His gaze found Floppy Jowls just as that worthy left his seat, mug in hand, and joined him at the table.

The latter's move in apparently welcoming the newcomer made the tension disappear. The others lost interest in Mowry, the bar attendant lounged back, and general conversation was resumed. It showed that Floppy Jowls was well-known among the hard-faced clientele; they'd accept anyone he knew.

Meanwhile, he had squatted face to face with Mowry and introduced himself with, 'My name is Urhava, Butin Urhava.' He

59

paused, waiting for a response that did not come, then went on. 'You're a stranger. From Diracta. Specifically from Masham. I can tell by your accent.'

'Clever of you,' Mowry encouraged.

'One has to be clever to get by. The stupid don't.' He took a swig of *zith*. 'You wouldn't walk into this place unless you were a genuine stranger – or one of the Kaitempi.'

'No?'

'No. And the Kaitempi wouldn't send just one man in here. They'd send six. Maybe more. The Kaitempi would expect trouble aplenty in the Café Susun.'

'That,' said Mowry, 'suits me very well.'

'It suits me even better.' Butin Urhava showed the snout of Sallana's gun over the edge of the table. It was pointed straight at Mowry's middle. 'I do not like being followed. If this gun went off, nobody here but you would give a damn. So you'd better talk. Why have you been following me, *hi?*'

'You knew I was behind you all the time?'

'I did. What's the idea?'

'You'll hardly believe it when I tell you.' Leaning across the table, Mowry grinned straight into Urhava's scowling face. 'I want to give you a thousand guilders.'

'That's nice,' said Urhava, unimpressed. 'That's very nice.' His eyes narrowed. 'And you're all set to reach into your pocket and give it to me, *hi?*'

Mowry nodded, still grinning. 'Yes – unless you're so lily-livered that you prefer to reach into it yourself.'

'You won't bait me that way,' retorted Urhava. 'I've got control of the situation and I'm keeping it, see? Now get busy dipping – but if what comes out of that pocket is a gun, it's *you* and not me who'll be the wrong end of the bang.'

With the weapon steadily centred upon him over the table's rim, Mowry felt in his right-hand pocket, drew out a neat wad of twenty-guilder notes, and poked them across the table. 'There you are. They're all yours.'

For a moment, Urhava gaped with complete incredulity;

then he made a swift pass, and the notes vanished. The gun also disappeared. He leaned back in his seat and studied Mowry with a mixture of bafflement and suspicion. 'Now show me the string.'

'No string,' Mowry assured him. 'Just a gift from an admirer.'

'Meaning who?'

'Me.'

'But you don't know me from the Statue of Jaime.'

'I hope to,' said Mowry. 'I hope to know you well enough to convince you of something mighty important.'

'And that is what?'

'There's lots more money where that came from.'

'Is that so?' Urhava gave a knowing smirk. 'Well, where did it come from?'

'I just told you – an admirer.'

'Don't give me that.'

'All right. The conversation is over. It's been nice knowing you. Now get back to your own seat.'

'Don't be silly.' Licking his lips, Urhava reduced his voice to a whisper. 'How much?'

'Twenty thousand guilders.'

The other fanned his hands as if beating off an annoying fly. 'Sh-h-h! Don't say it so loud!' He looked around the room cautiously. 'Did you actually say *twenty thousand?*'

'Yar.'

Urhava took a deep breath. 'Who d'you want killed?'

'One – for a start.'

'Are you serious?'

'I've just given you a thousand gilders, and that's not a joke. Besides, you can put the matter to the test. Cut a throat and collect – it's as easy as that.'

'Just for a start, you said?'

'I did. By that is meant that if I like your work I'll offer further employment. I've got a list of names and will pay twenty thousand per corpse.'

Watching Urhava for effect, James Mowry put a note of

warning into his voice. 'The Kaitempi will reward you with ten thousand for delivering me into their hands, no risk attached. But to get it, you sacrifice all chance at a far bigger sum – maybe a million or more.' He paused. 'One does not flood one's own gold mine, does one?'

'Nar, not unless one is cracked.' Urhava became slightly unnerved as his thoughts milled around. 'And what makes you think I'm a professional killer?'

'I don't. But I know you probably have a police record; otherwise, you wouldn't have swiped that gun. Nor would you be known in a joint like this. That means you're either the type who can do some dirty work for me or can introduce me to someone willing to do it. Personally, I don't care a hoot who does it. The point is that I reek of money, and you love the scent of it. If you want to go on sniffing it, you've got to do something about it.'

Urhava nodded slowly; he stuck a hand in his pocket and fondled the thousand guilders. There was a queer fire in his eyes. 'I don't do that kind of work; it's not quite in my line. And it needs more than one, but . . .'

'But what?'

'Not saying. I've got to have time to think this over. I want to discuss it with a couple of friends.'

Mowry stood up. 'I'll give you four days to find them and chew it over. By then you'd better have made up your mind one way or another. I'll be here again in four days' time at this hour.' Then he gave the other a light but imperative shove. '*I* don't like being followed either. Lay off if you want to grow old and get rich.'

With that, he departed.

SIX

In the early morning Mowry went to a different agency and rented a dynocar under the name of Morfid Payth with an address in Radine. He couldn't risk using the same agency twice in succession; it was very likely that already the police had visited the first one and asked pointed questions. There they'd recognize him as the subject of official investigation and detain him on some pretext while they used the telephone.

He drove out of the town carefully, not wanting to draw the attention of any patrol-cars lurking around. Eventually he reached the tree with the abnormal branch formation and the mock-tombstone beneath it. For a few minutes he stopped nearby, pretending to tinker with the dynamo until the road was clear of traffic. Then he drove the car over the grass verge and in between the trees.

After that he went back on foot and satisfied himself that the car could not be seen from the road. With his feet he scuffed the grass, concealing the tire tracks that entered the forest. That done, he headed for the distant cave.

He got there in the late afternoon. When still deep among the trees, and eight hundred yards from his destination, the ornamental ring on the middle finger of his left hand started tingling. The sensation grew progressively stronger as he neared; he made a straight and confident approach, with no preliminary skirmishing. The ring would not have tingled if Container-22 had ceased to radiate, and that would happen only if its beam were broken by something man-sized entering the cave.

And in the cave was something more spectacular than an invisible warning system. It was a reasonable assumption that any discoverers would start prying open the stacked duralumin cylinders, including Container-30. When they interfered with that one, the resulting bang would be heard and felt in faraway Pertane.

Once in the cave, James Mowry opened Container-2, got busy while daylight lasted, and treated himself to a real Earth-meal concocted of real Earth-food. He was far from being a gourmet, but shared with exiles a delight in the flavours of home. A small can of pineapple seemed like a taste of heaven; he lingered over every drop of juice, and made it last twenty minutes. The treat boosted his morale, and made Terra's forces out there among the stars seem less far away.

Upon the fall of darkness, he rolled Container-5 out the cave's mouth and upended it on the tiny beach. It was now a tall, silver-gray cylinder pointed at the stars. From its side he unclipped a small handle, stuck it into a hole in the slight blister near the base and wound vigorously. Something inside began to murmur a smooth and steady *zuum-zuum*.

He now took the top cap off the cylinder, having to stand on tiptoe to get at it; then he sat on a nearby rock and waited. After the cylinder had warmed up, it emitted a sharp click and the *zuum-zuum* struck into a deeper note. He knew that it was now shouting into space, using soundless words far stronger and more penetrating than those of any spoken language.

Whirrup-dzzt-pam! Whirrup-dzzt-pam!

'Jaimec calling! Jaimec calling!'

Now he could do nothing but wait. The call was not being directed straight to Terra, which was much too far away to permit a conversation with only brief time-lags. Mowry was calling a spatial listening-post and field headquarters near enough to be on – or perhaps actually within – the rim of the Sirian Empire. He did not know its precise location; as Wolf said, what he didn't know he couldn't tell.

A prompt response was unlikely. Out there, they'd be

listening for a hundred calls on as many frequencies, and they'd be held on some of them while messages passed to and fro.

Nearly three hours crawled by while the cylinder stood on the pebble beach and gave forth its scarcely audible *zuum-zuum*. Then suddenly a tiny red eye glowed bright and winked steadily near its top.

Again, Mowry strained on tiptoe, cursing his shortness; he felt into the cylinder's open top and took out what looked exactly like an ordinary telephone. Holding it to his ear, he said into the mouthpiece, 'JM on Jaimec.'

It was a few minutes before the response came back – a voice that seemed to be speaking through a load of gravel. But it was a Terran voice speaking English. It said, 'Ready to tape your report. Fire away.'

Mowry tried to sit down while he talked, but found the connecting cord too short; he had to stand. In this position, he recited as fast as he could. *The Tale of a Wasp*, by Samuel Sucker, he thought wryly. He gave full details and again had to wait quite a while.

Then the voice rasped. 'Good! You're doing fine!'

'Am I? Can't see any signs of it so far. I've been plastering paper all over the planet and nothing is happening.'

'Plenty is happening,' contradicted the voice. It came through with a rhythmic variation in amplitude as it foiled Sirian detection devices by switching five times per second, through a chain of differently positioned transmitters. 'You just can't see the full picture from where you're standing.'

'How about giving me a glimpse?'

'The pot is coming slowly but surely to the boil. Their fleets are being widely dispersed, there are vast troop movements from their overcrowded home-system to the outer planets of their empire. They're gradually being chivvied into a fix. They can't hold what they've got without spreading all over it. The wider they spread the thinner they get. The thinner they get, the easier it is to bite lumps out of them. Hold it a bit while I check your bailiwick.' He went off, came back after a time.

'Yes, the position there is that they daren't take any strength away from Jaimec, no matter how greatly needed elsewhere. In fact, they may yet have to add to it at the expense of Diracta. You're the cause of that.'

'Sweet of you to say so,' said Mowry. A thought struck him and he said eagerly, 'Hey, who gave you that information?'

'Monitoring and Decoding Service. They dig a lot out of enemy broadcasts.'

'Oh.' He felt disappointed, having hoped for news of a Terran Intelligence agent somewhere on Jaimec. But, of course, they wouldn't tell him. They'd give him no information that Kaitempi persuasion might force out of him. 'How about this Kaitempi card and embossing machine? Do I leave them here to be collected, or do I keep them for myself?'

'Stand by and I'll find out.' The voice went away for more than an hour, returned with, 'Sorry about the delay . . . You can keep that stuff and use it as you think best. TI got a card recently. An agent bought one for them.'

'*Bought one?*' He waggled his eyebrows in surprise.

'Yes – with his life. What did yours cost?'

'Major Sallana's life, as I told you.'

'Tsk-tsk! Those cards come mighty dear.' There was a pause, then. 'Closing down. Best of luck!'

'Thanks!'

With some reluctance, Mowry replaced the receiver, switched off the *zuum-zuum*, capped the cylinder, and rolled it back into the cave. He'd have liked to listen until dawn to anything that maintained the invisible tie between him and that faraway life form. 'Best of luck!' the voice had said, not knowing how much more it meant than the alien, 'Live long!'

From yet another container he took several packets and small parcels, distributed them about his person, and put others into a canvas shoulder bag of the kind favoured by the Sirian peasantry. Being now more familiar with the forest, he felt sure he could fumble his way through it in the dark. The going would be tougher, the journey would take longer, but he could not resist the urge to get back to the car as soon as possible.

Before leaving, his last act was to press the hidden button on Container-22, which had ceased to radiate the moment he'd entered the cave and remained dead ever since. After a one-minute delay, it would again set up the invisible barrier.

He got out of the cave fast, the parcels heavy around him, and had made thirty yards into the trees when his finger-ring started its tingling. Slowly he moved on, feeling his way from time to time. The tingling gradually weakened with distance, faded out after eight hundred yards.

From then on, he consulted his luminous compass at least a hundred times. It led him back to the road at a point half a mile from the car, a pardonable margin of error in a twenty-mile journey, two-thirds of which had been in darkness.

The day of James Mowry's appointment with Butin Urhava started with a highly significant event. Over the radio and video, through the public-address system, and in all the newspapers the government came out with the same announcement. Mowry heard the muffled bellowings of a loudspeaker two streets away, and the shrill cries of news vendors. He bought a paper and read it over his breakfast.

Under the War Emergency Powers Act, by order of the Jaimec Ministry of Defence: all organizations, societies, parties, and other corporate bodies will be registered at the Central Bureau of Records, Pertane, not later than the twentieth of this month. Secretaries will state in full the objects and purposes of their respective organizations, societies, parties, or other corporate bodies, give the address of habitual meeting places, and provide a complete list of members.

Under the War Emergency Powers Act, by order of the Jaimec Ministry of Defence: after the twentieth of this month, any organization, society, party, or other corporate

67

body will be deemed an illegal movement if not registered in accordance with the above order. Membership in an illegal movement, or the giving of aid and comfort to any member of an illegal movement, will constitute a treacherous offence punishable by death.

So at last they'd made a countermove. *Dirac Angestun Gesept* must kneel at the confessional or at the strangling post. By a simple legislative trick they'd got *DAG* where they wanted it, coming and going. It was a kill-or-cure tactic, full of psychological menace, well calculated to scare all the weaklings out of *DAG*'s ranks.

Weaklings talk; they betray their fellows, one by one, right through the chain of command to the top. They represent the rot that spreads through a system and brings it to total collapse. In theory, anyway.

Mowry read the proclamation again, grinning to himself and enjoying every word. The government was going to have a tough time enticing informers from the *DAG*. A fat lot of talking can be done by a membership completely unaware of its status.

For instance, Butin Urhava was a fully paid-up member in good standing – and didn't know it. The Kaitempi could trap him and draw out his innards very, very slowly without gaining one worthwhile word about the Sirian Freedom Party.

Around midday, Mowry looked in at the Central Bureau of Records. Sure enough, a line stretched from the door to the counter, where a pair of disdainful officials were passing out forms. The line slowly edged forward. It was composed of secretaries, or other officers, of trade guilds, *zith*-drinking societies, video fan clubs, and every other conceivable kind of organization. The skinny oldster moping in the rear was Area Supervisor of the Pan-Sirian Association of Lizard Watchers; the pudgy specimen one step ahead of him represented the Pertane Model Rocket Builders Club.

Joining the line, Mowry said conversationally to Skinny, 'Nuisance this, isn't it?'

'Yar. Only the Statue of Jaime knows why it is considered necessary.'

'Maybe they're trying to round up people with special talents,' Mowry suggested. 'Radio experts, photographers, and people like that. They can use all sorts of technicians in wartime.'

'They could have said so in plain words,' opined Skinny impatiently. 'They could have published a list of them and ordered them to report in.'

'Yar, that's right.'

'My group watches lizards. Of what special use is a lizard-watcher, *hi?*'

'I can't imagine. Why watch lizards, anyway?'

'Have *you* ever watched them?'

'No,' admitted Mowry, without shame.

'Then you don't know the fascination of it.'

Pudgy turned round and said with a superior air, 'My group builds model rockets.'

'Kid stuff,' defined Skinny.

'That's what you think. I'll have you know that every member is a potential rocket engineer, and in time of war a rocket engineer is a valuable . . .'

'Move up,' said Skinny, nudging him. They shuffled forward, stopped. Skinny said to Mowry, 'What's your crowd do?'

'We etch glass.'

'Well, that's a high form of art. I have seen some very attractive examples of it myself. They were luxury articles, though. A bit beyond the common purse.' He let go a loud sniff. 'What good are glass-etchers for winning battles?'

'You guess,' Mowry invited.

'Now take rockets,' put in Pudgy. 'The rocket is essential to space-war, and . . .'

'Move up,' ordered Skinny again.

They reached the stack of forms and were each given one off the top. The group dispersed, going their various ways while a long line of later comers edged toward the counter. Mowry went to the main post office, sat at a vacant table, and started to fill out the form. He got some satisfaction out of doing it with a government pen and government ink.

Title of organization: *Dirac Angestun Gesept.*
Purpose of organization: *Destruction of present government and termination of war against Terra.*
Customary meeting place: *Wherever Kaitempi can't find us.*
Names and addresses of elected officers: *You'll find out when it's too late.*
Attach hereto complete list of members: *Nar.*
Signature: *Jaime Shalapurta.*

That last touch was a calculated insult to the much revered Statue of Jaime; loosely translated, it meant James Stoney-bottom.

He was about to mail the form back to the Bureau when it occurred to him to jazz it up still more. Forthwith he took the form to his room, shoved it into the embossing machine and impressed it with the Kaitempi cartouche. Then he posted it.

This performance pleased him immensely. A month ago the recipients would have dismissed it as the work of an imbecile. But today the circumstances were vastly different. The powers that be had revealed themselves as annoyed, if not frightened. With moderate luck, the sardonic registration-form would boost their anger, and that would be all to the good; a mind filled with fury cannot think in cool, logical manner.

When one is fighting a paper-war, Mowry thought, one uses paper-war tactics that in the long run can be just as lethal as high explosive. And the tactics are not limited in scope by use of one material. Paper can convey a private warning, a public threat, secret temptation, open defiance, wall-bills, window-stickers, leaflets dropped by the thousands from the roof-tops, cards left on seats or slipped into pockets and purses . . . *money.*

Yes, money. With paper money he could buy a lot of the deeds needed to back up the words.

At the proper hour, James Mowry set out for the Café Susun.

Not having yet received the *DAG*'s thumb-on-nose registration, the Jaimecan authorities were still able to think in a calculating and menacing way. Their countermoves had not been confined to that morning's new law. They had taken matters further by concocting the snap search.

It almost caught Mowry at the first grab. He was heading for his rendezvous when suddenly a line of uniformed police extended itself across the street. A second line appeared simultaneously four hundred yards farther on. From the dumbfounded mob trapped between the lines appeared a number of plain-clothes members of the Kaitempi; these at once commenced a swift and expert search of everyone thus halted in the street. Meanwhile, both lines of police kept their full attention inward, watching to see that nobody ducked into a doorway, or bolted through a house to escape the mass search.

Thanking his lucky stars that he was outside the trap, and being ignored, James Mowry faded into the background as inconspicuously as possible and beat it home fast. In his room, he burned all documents relating to Shir Agavan and crumbled the ashes into fine dust. That identity was now dead.

From one of his packages, he took a new set of papers swearing before all and sundry that he was Krag Wulkin, special correspondent of a leading news agency, with a home address on Diracta. In some ways, it was a better camouflage than the former one; it lent added plausibility to his Mashambi accent. Moreover, a complete check on it would involve wasting a month referring back to the Sirian home planet.

Thus armed, he started out again. Though better fitted to face awkward questions, the risk of being asked them had been greatly boosted by the snap-search technique; he took to the streets with the feeling that, somehow or other, the hunters at last had picked up the scent.

There was no way of telling exactly what the searchers were seeking. Maybe they were trying to catch people carrying subversive propaganda on their persons; perhaps they were looking for people with *DAG* membership cards; or could be they were haphazardly groping around for a dynocar renter named Shir Agavan. Anyway, the tactic proved that someone among Jaimec's big wheels had become very irritated.

Luckily, no more traps opened in his path before he reached the Café Susun. He went in, found Urhava and two others seated at the far table, half-concealed in dim light, where they could keep watch on the door.

'You're late,' greeted Urhava. 'We thought you weren't coming.'

'I got delayed by a police raid on the street. The cops looked surly. You fellows just robbed a bank or something?'

'No, we haven't.' Urhava made a casual gesture toward his companions. 'Meet Gurd and Skriva.'

Mowry acknowledged them with a curt nod and looked them over. They were much alike, obviously brothers – flat-faced, and hard-eyed, with pinned-back ears that came up to sharp points. Each looked capable of selling the other into slavery, provided there was no comeback with a knife.

'We haven't heard *your* name,' said Gurd, speaking between long, narrow teeth.

'You aren't going to, either,' responded Mowry.

Gurd bristled. 'Why not?'

'Because you don't really care what my name is,' Mowry told him. 'If your neck is safe, it's a matter of total indifference to you *who* gives you a load of guilders.'

'Yar, that's right,' chipped in Skriva, his eyes glittering. 'Money is money, regardless of who hands it over. Shut up, Gurd.'

'I only wanted to know,' mumbled Gurd, subdued.

Urhava took over with the mouth-watering eagerness of one

on the make. 'I've given these boys your proposition. They're interested.' He turned to them. 'Aren't you?'

'Yar,' said Skriva. He concentrated attention upon Mowry. 'You want someone in his meat-crate. That right?'

'I want someone stone cold, and I don't give a hoot whether or not he is crated.'

'We can tend to that.' Skriva put on his toughest expression, which told all and sundry that he'd kilt him a b'ar when he wuz only three. Then he said, 'For fifty thousand.'

Mowry stood up and ambled toward the door. 'Live long!'

'Come back!' Skriva shot to his feet, waved urgently. Urhava had the appalled look of someone suddenly cut out of a rich uncle's will. Gurd sucked his teeth with visible agitation.

Pausing at the door, Mowry held it open. 'You stupes ready to talk sense?'

'Sure,' pleaded Skriva. 'I was only joking. Come back and sit down.'

'Bring us four *ziths*,' said Mowry to the attendant behind the counter. He returned to the table, resumed his seat. 'No more bad jokes. I don't appreciate them.'

'Forget it,' advised Skriva. 'We've got a couple of questions for you.'

'You may voice them,' agreed Mowry. He accepted a mug of *zith* from the attendant, paid him, took a swig and eyed Skriva with becoming lordliness.

Skriva said, 'Who d'you want us to slap down? And how do we know we're going to get our money?'

'For the first, the victim is Colonel Hage-Ridarta.' He scribbled rapidly on a piece of paper, gave it to the other. 'That is his address.'

'I see.' Skriva stared at the slip. 'And the money?'

'I'll pay you five thousand right now, as an act of faith, and fifteen thousand when the job is done.' He stopped and gave the three a cold, forbidding eye. 'I don't take your word for the doing. It's got to be squawked on the news channels before I part with another one-tenth guilder.'

'You trust us a lot, don't you?' said Skriva, scowling.

'No more than I have to.'

'Same applies on this side.'

'Look,' Mowry urged, 'we've *got* to play ball with each other. Here's how. I've got a list. If you do the first job for me and I renege, you're not going to do the others, are you?'

'No.'

'What's more, you'll take it out of my hide first chance you get, won't you?'

'You can bet on that,' said Gurd.

'Similarly, if you pull a fast one on me, you will cut yourselves out of big money. I'm outbidding the Kaitempi by a large margin, see? Don't you fellows *want* to get rich?'

'I hate the idea of it,' said Skriva. 'Let's see that five thousand.'

Mowry slipped him the package under the table. The three checked it in their laps. After a while, Skriva looked up, his face slightly flushed.

'We're sold. Who is this Hage-Ridarta *soko?*'

'Just a brass hat who has lived too long.'

That was a half-truth. Hage-Ridarta was listed in the city directory as an officer commanding an outfit of space marines. But his name had been appended to an authoritative letter in the late Major Sallana's files. The tone of the letter had been that of a boss to an underling. Hage-Ridarta was an officially disguised occupant of the Kaitempi top bracket.

'Why d'you want him out of the way?' demanded Gurd.

Before Mowry could reply, Skriva said fiercely, 'I told you before to shut up. I'll handle this. Can't you button your trap even for twenty thousand?'

'We haven't got it yet,' persisted Gurd.

'You will get it,' Mowry soothed. 'And more, lots more. The day the news of Hage-Ridarta's death is given in the papers, or on the radio, I'll be here at this same time in the evening with fifteen thousand guilders and the next name. If by any chance

I'm held up and can't make it, I'll be here at the same time the following evening.'

'You'd better be!' informed Gurd, glowering.

Urhava had a question of his own. 'What's my percentage for introducing the boys?'

'I don't know.' Mowry turned to Skriva. 'How much do you intend to give him?'

'Who? . . . Me?' Skriva was taken aback.

'Yes, you. The gentleman thirsts for a rake-off. You don't expect me to pay him, do you? Think I'm made of money?'

'Somebody had better fork out,' declared Urhava. 'Or . . .'

Skriva shoved scowling features up against him and breathed over his face, 'Or *what?*'

'Nothing,' said Urhava. 'Nothing at all.'

'That's better,' Skriva approved in grating tones. 'That's a whole lot better. Just sit around and be a good boy, Butin, and we'll feed you crumbs from our table. Get fidgety, and you'll soon find yourself in no condition to eat them. In fact, you won't be able to swallow. It's tough when a fellow can't swallow. You wouldn't like that, would you, Butin?'

Saying nothing, Urhava sat still. His complexion was slightly mottled.

Repeating the face-shoving act, Skriva shouted, 'I just asked you a civil question. I said you wouldn't like it, would you?'

'No,' admitted Urhava, tilting back his chair to get away from the face.

Mowry decided that the time had come to leave this happy scene. He took his daring far enough to say to Skriva, 'Don't get tough ideas about *me* – if you want to stay in business.'

With that, he departed. He did not worry about the possibility of any of them following him. They wouldn't offend the best customer they'd had since crime came to Pertane.

As he walked rapidly along, he pondered the evening's work and decided it had been a wise move to insist that money did not grow on trees. They'd have shown no respect whatsoever if he'd been willing to shovel it out regardless as, in fact, he could afford to do should the necessity arise. They'd have put on maximum pressure to gain the most in return for the least, and that would have produced more arguments than results.

It was also a good thing that he'd refused a cut to Urhava, and left them to fight it out between themselves. The reaction had been revealing. A mob, even a small mob, is only as strong as its weakest link. It was important to discover a prospective squealer before it was too late. In this respect, Butin Urhava hadn't shown up so well.

'Somebody had better fork out or . . .'

The testing time would come soon after he'd paid over fifteen thousand guilders for a job well done, and those concerned divided the loot. Well, if the situation seemed to justify it, that's when he'd give the Gurd-Skriva brothers the next name – Butin Urhava.

He continued homeward, deep in thought and not looking where he was going. He had just reached the conclusion that Urhava's throat would have to be slit sooner or later, when a heavy hand clamped on his shoulder and a voice rasped, 'Lift them up, Dreamy, and let's see what you've got in your pockets. Come on, you're not deaf – lift 'em, I said!'

With a sense of shock, Mowry raised his arms and felt fingers start prying into his clothes. Nearby, forty or fifty equally surprised walkers were holding the same pose. A line of phlegmatic police stood across the street a hundred yards away; in the opposite direction a second line looked on with the same indifference. Again the random trap had sprung.

SEVEN

A flood of superfast thoughts raced through James Mowry's startled brain as he stood with arms extended above his head. Thank heavens he'd got rid of that money; they'd have been unpleasantly inquisitive about so large a sum being carried in one lump. If they were looking for Shir Agavan, they were out of luck. In any case, he wasn't going to let them take him in, even for questioning. It would be better at the last resort to break this searcher's neck and run like blazes.

'If the cops shoot me down, it'll be a quicker and easier end. When Terra gets no more signals from me, Wolf will choose my successor and feed the poor sap the same . . .'

'*Hi?*' The Kaitempi agent broke his train of thought by holding Mowry's wallet open and gazing with surprise at Sallana's card reposing therein. The tough expression faded from his heavy features as if wiped away. 'One of us? An officer?' He took a closer look. 'But I do not recognize *you.*'

'You wouldn't,' said Mowry, showing just the right degree of arrogance. 'I arrived only today from HQ on Diracta.' He pulled a face. 'And this is the reception I get.'

'It cannot be helped,' apologized the agent. 'The revolutionary movement must be suppressed at all costs, and it's as big a menace here as on any other planet. You know how things are on Diracta – well, they're not one whit better on Jaimec.'

'It won't last,' Mowry responded, speaking with authority. 'On Diracta we expect to make a complete clean-up in the near future. After that, you won't have much trouble here. When you cut off the head, the body dies.'

'I hope you're right. The Spakum war is enough without an army of traitors sniping in the rear.' The agent closed the wallet and gave it back. His other hand held the Krag Wulkin documents, at which he had not yet looked. Waiting for Mowry to pocket the wallet, he returned the remaining material and said jocularly, 'Here are your false papers.'

'Nothing is false that has been officially issued,' said Mowry, frowning in disapproval.

'No, I suppose not. I hadn't thought of it in that light.' The agent backed off. 'Sorry to have troubled you. I suggest you call at local headquarters as soon as possible and have them circulate your photo, so that you'll be known to us. Otherwise, you may be stopped and searched repeatedly.'

'I'll do that,' promised Mowry, unable to imagine anything he'd less intention of doing.

'You'll excuse me – I must tend to these others.' So saying, the agent attracted the attention of the nearest police, pointed to Mowry. Then he made for a sour-faced civilian who was standing nearby waiting to be frisked. Reluctantly the civilian lifted his arms.

Mowry walked toward the line of police, which opened and let him pass through. At such moments, he thought, one is supposed to be cool, radiating supreme self-confidence in all directions. He wasn't like that at all; on the contrary, he was weak in the knees and had a sick feeling. He had to force himself to continue steadily onward with what appeared to be absolute nonchalance.

He made six hundred yards and reached the next corner before some warning instinct made him look back. Police were still blocking the road, but beyond them four of the Kaitempi had clustered together in conversation. One of them, the agent who had released Mowry, pointed his way. There followed what appeared to be ten seconds of heated argument before they reached a decision.

'Stop him!'

The nearest police turned around, startled, seeking a fleeing quarry. Mowry's legs became filled with an almost irresistible urge to get going. He forced them to maintain their steady pace.

There were a number of people in the street, some merely hanging around and gaping at the trap, others walking the same way as Mowry. Most of the latter wanted no part of what was going on higher up the road, and considered it expedient to amble somewhere else. James Mowry kept with them, showing no great hurry. That baffled the police; for a few valuable seconds they stayed put, hands on weapons, while they sought in vain for visible evidence of guilt.

It provided sufficient delay to enable him to get round the corner and out of sight. At that point, the shouting Kaitempi realized that the police were stalled; they lost patience and broke into a furious sprint. Half a dozen clumping cops immediately raced with them.

Overtaking a youth who was sauntering dozily along, Mowry gave him an urgent shove in the back. 'Quick! – they're after you! The Kaitempi!'

'I've done nothing. I . . .'

'How long will it take to convince them of that? *Run*, you fool!'

The other used up a few moments gaping before he heard the oncoming rush of heavy feet, the shouts of pursuers nearing the corner. He lost colour and tore down the road at a velocity that paid tribute to his innocence. He'd have overtaken and passed a bolting jack rabbit with no trouble at all.

Entering an adjacent shop, Mowry threw a swift look around to see what it sold and said casually, 'I wish ten of those small cakes with the toasted-nut tops, and . . .'

The arm of the law thundered round the corner, fifty strong. The hunt roared past the shop, its leaders baying with triumph as they spotted the distant figure of the man who had done nothing. Mowry stared in dumb amazement. The corpulent Sirian behind the counter eyed the window with sad resignation.

'What is happening?' asked Mowry.

'They're after someone,' diagnosed Fatso. He sighed and rubbed his protruding belly. 'Always they are after someone. What a world! What a war!'

'Makes you tired, *hi?*'

'Aie, yar! Every day, every minute there is something. Last night, according to news channels, they destroyed the main Spakum space-fleet for the tenth time. Today they are pursuing the remnants of what is said to have been destroyed. For months we have been making triumphant retreats before a demoralized enemy who is advancing in utter disorder.' He made a sweeping motion with a pudgy hand. It indicated disgust. 'I am fat, as you can see. That makes me an idiot. You wish . . . ?'

'Ten of those small cakes with the toasted-nut . . .'

A belated cop pounded past the window. He was two hundred yards behind the pack and breathless. As he thudded along, he let go a couple of shots in the air.

'See what I mean?' said Fatso. 'You wish . . . ?'

'Ten of those small cakes with the toasted-nut tops. I also wish to order a special celebration-cake to be supplied five days hence. Perhaps you can show me some samples, or help me with suggestions, *hi?*'

He managed to waste twenty minutes within the shop and the time was well worth the few guilders it cost. Twenty minutes, he estimated, would be just enough time to permit local excitement to die down while the pursuit continued elsewhere.

Halfway home, he was tempted to donate the cakes to a mournful-looking cop, but refrained. The more he had to dodge authority's frantic fly-swattings, the harder it was to behave like a wasp and get a laugh out of it.

Within his room he flopped, fully dressed, on the bed and summarized the day's doings. He had escaped a trap, but only by the skin of his teeth. It proved that such traps were escapable – but not forever. What had made them take after him? He guessed it was the intervention of an officious character who had noticed him walking through the cordon.

'Who's that you've let go?'

'An officer, Captain.'

'What d'you mean, an officer?'

'A Kaitempi officer, Captain. I do not know him, but he had a correct card. He said that he had just been drafted from Diracta.'

'A card, *hi*? Did you notice its serial number?'

'I had no particular reason to remember it, Captain. It was obviously genuine. But let me see . . . yar . . . it was SXB80313. Or perhaps SXB80131. I am not sure which.'

'Major Sallana's card was SXB80131. You half-witted *soko*, you may have had his killer in your hands!'

'*Stop him!*'

Now, by virtue of the fact that he had evaded capture, plus the fact that he had failed to turn up at headquarters to gain photographic identification, they'd assume that Sallana's slayer really had been in the net. Previously, they had not known where to start looking, other than within the ranks of the elusive *DAG*. But now they knew the killer was in Pertane; they had a description of him; and one Kaitempi agent could be relied upon to recognize him on sight.

In other words, the heat was on. Henceforth, in Pertane at least, the going would be tougher, with the pressure-cell and the strangling-post looming ever nearer. James Mowry groaned as he thought of it. He had never asked much of life, and would have been quite satisfied merely to sprawl on a golden throne and be fawned upon by sycophants. To be dropped down a Sirian-dug hole, dead cold and dyed purple, was to take things too much to the opposite extreme.

But to counterbalance this dismal prospect there was something heartening – a snatch of conversation.

'The revolutionary movement . . . as big a menace here as on any other planet. You know how things are on Diracta – well, they're not one whit better on Jaimec.'

That told him plenty; it revealed that *Dirac Angestun Gesept* was not merely a Wolf-concocted nightmare designed to disturb the sleep of Jaimecan politicos. It was empire-wide, covering more than a hundred planets, its strength – or rather its pseudo-strength – greatest on the home-world of Diracta, the nerve centre and beating heart of the entire Sirian species. It was more than a hundred times greater than had appeared to Mowry in his purely localized endeavours.

To the Sirian powers that be, *DAG* was a major peril, hacking down the back door while the Terrans were busily bashing in the front one. Other wasps were at work . . .

Somebody in the Sirian High Command – a psychologist or a cynic – decided that the more one chivvied the civilian population, the lower its morale sank. The constant stream of new emergency orders, regulations, restrictions, the constant police and Kaitempi activity, stoppings, searchings, questionings all tended to create that dull, pessimistic resignation demonstrated by Fatso in the cake shop. An antidote was needed.

Accordingly a show was put on. The radio, video, and newspapers combined to strike up the band and draw the crowds.

GREAT VICTORY IN CENTAURI SECTOR

Yesterday powerful Terran space-forces became trapped in the region of A. Centauri, and a fierce battle raged as they tried to break out. The Sirian fourth, sixth, and seventh fleets, manœuvering in masterly manner, frustrated all their efforts to get free and escape. Many casualties were inflicted upon the enemy. Precise figures are not yet available, but the latest report from the area of conflict states that we have lost four battleships and one light cruiser, the crews of which have all been rescued. More than seventy Terran warships have been destroyed.

And so the story went on, for minutes of time and columns of print, complete with pictures of the battleship *Hashim*; the heavy cruiser *Jaimec*; some members of their crews when home on leave a year ago; Rear-Admiral Pent-Gurhana saluting a prosperous navy contractor; the Statue of Jaime casting its shadow across a carefully positioned Terran banner, and – loveliest touch of all – a five-centuries-old photograph of a scowling, bedraggled bunch of Mongolian bandits authoritatively described as 'Terran space-troops whom we snatched from death as their stricken ship plunged sunward.'

One columnist, graciously admitting lack of facts and substituting so-called expert knowledge, devoted half a page to a lurid description of how heroic space-marines had performed the snatch-from-death *in vacuo*. How fortunate were the vile Terrans, he proclaimed, in finding themselves opposed by so daring and gallant a foe. At which point he gave way to KWIK, the wonder cure for aching bellies.

Mowry couldn't decide whether casualty figures had been reversed, or whether a fight had taken place at all. Dismissing it with a sniff of disdain, he sought through the rest of the paper and found a small item on the back page.

Colonel Hage-Ridarta, officer commanding 77 Company SM, was found dead in his car at midnight last night. He had been shot through the head. A gun was lying nearby. Suicide is not suspected and police investigations are continuing.

So the Gurd-Skriva combination worked mighty fast; they'd done the job within a few hours of taking it on. Yar, money was a wonderful thing, especially when Terran engravers and presses could produce it in unlimited supply with little trouble and at small cost.

This unexpected promptness set James Mowry a new problem. To get more such action he'd have to pay up, and thereby risk falling into another trap while on the way to the rendezvous. Right now, he dare not show Sallana's card in Pertane, though it might prove useful elsewhere. His documents for Krag Wulkin, special correspondent, might possibly get him out of a jam – provided the trappers didn't search further, find him loaded with guilders, and ask difficult questions.

Within an hour, the High Command solved the problem for him. They put on the circus in the form of a victory parade. To the beat and blare of a dozen bands, a great column of troops, tanks, guns, mobile radar units, flame-throwers, rocket-batteries and gas-projectors, tracked recovery vehicles, and other paraphernalia crawled into Pertane from the west, tramped and rumbled toward the east.

Helicopters and jet planes swooped at low level, and a small number of nimble space-scouts thundered at great altitude. Citizens by the thousands lined the streets and cheered more from habit than from genuine enthusiasm.

This, Mowry realized, was his heaven-sent opportunity. Snap searches might continue down the side streets, and in the city's tough quarters, but they'd be well-nigh impossible on the east-west artery, with all that military traffic passing through. If he could reach the cross-town route, he could get out of Pertane in safety.

He paid his miserly landlord two months' rent in advance without creating more than joyful surprise. Then he checked his false identity papers. Hurriedly he packed his bag with guilders, a fresh supply of stickers, a couple of small packages and got out.

No sudden traps opened out between there and the city centre; even if they ran around like mad, the police could not be everywhere at once. On the east-west road, he carried his bag unnoticed, being of less significance than a grain of sand amid the great mob of spectators that had assembled. By the same token, progress was difficult and slow.

Many of the shops he passed had boarded-up windows as evidence that they had been favoured by his propaganda. Others displayed new glass; on twenty-seven of these he slapped more stickers, while a horde of potential witnesses stood on tiptoe and stared over their fellows at the military procession. One sticker he plastered on a policeman's back, the broad, inviting stretch of black cloth proving irresistible.

Who will pay for this war?
Those who started it will pay.
With their money — and their lives.
Dirac Angestun Gesept.

After three hours of edging, pushing and some surreptitious sticker-planting, Mowry arrived at the city's outskirts. Here the tail end of the parade was still trundling noisily along. Standing spectators had thinned out, but a straggling group were walking in pace with the troops.

Around Mowry stood houses of a suburb too snooty to deserve the attentions of the police and Kaitempi; ahead stretched the open country and the road to Radine. He carried straight on, following the rearmost troops until the procession turned leftward and headed for the great military stronghold of Khamasta. Here, the accompanying civilians halted and watched them go, before returning to Pertane. Bag in hand, Mowry continued along the Radine road.

Moodiness afflicted him as he walked. He became obsessed with the notion that he had been chased out of the city, even if only temporarily, and he didn't like it. Every step he took seemed like another triumph for the foe, another defeat for himself.

At the training college they had lectured him again and again to the same effect: 'Maybe you *like* having a mulish character. Well, in some circumstances it's called courage; in others it's downright stupidity. You've got to resist the temptation to indulge in unprofitable heroics. Never abandon caution merely because you think it looks like cowardice. It requires guts to sacrifice one's ego for the sake of the job. A dead hero is of no use to us!'

Humph! easy for them to talk. He was still aggrieved when he reached a permasteel plaque standing by the roadside. It said: *Radine – 33 den.* He looked in both directions, found nobody in sight. Opening his bag, he took out a package and buried it at the base of the plaque.

EIGHT

That evening, James Mowry checked in at Radine's best and most expensive hotel. If the Jaimecan authorities had succeeded in following his tortuous trail around Pertane, they'd have noticed his penchant for hiding out in slum areas and tended to seek him in the planet's ratholes. With luck, a high-priced hotel would now be the last place in which they'd look for him. All the same, he'd have to be wary of the routine Kaitempi check of hotel registers.

Dumping his bag, he left the room at once; time was pressing. He hurried along the road, unworried about snap searches – which, for unknown reasons, were confined to the capital. Reaching a bank of public phone booths a mile from the hotel, he made a call to Pertane.

A sour voice answered, while the booth's tiny screen remained blank. 'Café Susun.'

'Skriva there?'

'Who wants him?'

'Me.'

'That tells me a lot. Why've you got that scanner switched off?'

'Listen, who's talking?' growled Mowry, eyeing his own faceless screen. 'You fetch Skriva and let him cope with his own troubles. You aren't his paid secretary, are you?'

There came a loud snort, a long silence, then Skriva's voice: 'Who's this?'

'Give me your pic and I'll give you mine.'

'I know who it is – I recognize the tones,' said Skriva. He switched his scanner; his unpleasing features gradually bloomed into the screen. Mowry switched likewise. Skriva frowned at him with dark suspicion. 'Thought you were going to meet us here. Why are you phoning?'

'I've been called out of town and can't get back for a while.'

'Is *that* so?'

'Yar, that *is* so!' snapped Mowry. 'And don't get tough with me because I won't stand for it, see?' He paused to let that sink in, then went on, 'You got a dyno?'

'Maybe,' said Skriva evasively.

'Can you leave right away?'

'Maybe.'

'If you want the goods, you can cut out the maybes and move fast.' Mowry held his phone before the scanner, tapped it suggestively and pointed to his ears to indicate that one never knew who was listening in these days. 'Get onto the Radine road and look under marker *33-den. Don't* take Urhava with you.'

'Hey, when will you . . .'

Mowry slammed down the phone, cutting off the other's irate query. Next he sought the local Kaitempi HQ, the address of which had been revealed in Major Sallana's secret correspondence.

He passed the building, keeping as far from it as possible on the other side of the street. He did not give close attention to the building itself, his gaze being concentrated above it. For the next hour he wandered around Radine with seeming aimlessness, still studying the areas above the rooftops.

Eventually satisfied, he looked for the city hall, found it, and repeated the process. He indulged in more erratic wandering from street to street, while apparently admiring the stars. Finally he returned to the hotel.

The next morning, he took a small package from his bag, pocketed it, and made straight for a large business block noted the previous evening. With a convincing air of self-assurance he entered the building and took the automatic elevator to the top floor. Here he found a dusty, seldom-used passage with a drop-ladder at one end.

There was nobody around. Even if somebody had come along, they might not have been unduly curious. Anyway, he had all his answers ready. Pulling down the ladder, he climbed it swiftly, got through the trap-door and onto the roof. From his package, Mowry took a tiny inductance coil fitted with clips and attached to a long, hair-thin cable with plug-in terminals at its other end.

Climbing a short trellis mast, he counted the wires on the telephone junction at its top, and checked the direction in which the seventh one ran. To this, he carefully fastened the coil. Then he descended, led the cable to the roof's edge, and gently paid it out until it was dangling full length into the road below. Its plug-in terminals were now swinging in the air at a point about four feet above the sidewalk.

Even as he looked down from the roof, half a dozen pedestrians passed the hanging cable and showed no interest in it. A couple of them glanced idly upward, saw somebody above, and wandered onward without remark. Nobody questions the activities of a man who clambers over roofs or disappears down grids in the street, provided he does it openly and with an air of quiet confidence.

He got down and out without mishap. Within an hour he had performed the same feat atop another building, and again got away unchallenged. The next move was to purchase another typewriter, paper, envelopes, and a small hand-printing set. It was still only midday when Mowry returned to his room and set to work as fast as he could go. He kept at it, without abatement, all that day, and most of the next day. When he had finished, the hand-printer and typewriter slid silently into the lake.

He now had in his case two hundred and twenty letters for future use; he had just mailed another two hundred and twenty to those who had received his first warning. The recipients, he hoped, would be far from charmed by the arrival of a second letter, with a third yet to come.

Hage-Ridarta was the second.
The list is long.
Dirac Angestun Gesept.

After lunch, he consulted yesterday's and today's news-papers at which he'd been too busy to look before now. The item he sought was not there: not a word about Butin Urhava. Momentarily, he wondered whether anything had gone wrong.

The general news was much as usual: victory still loomed nearer and nearer; casualties in the real or mythical Alpha Centauri battle were now officially confirmed at eleven Sirian warships, ninety-four Terran ones.

On an inner page, in an inconspicuous corner, it was announced that Sirian forces had abandoned the twin worlds of Fedira and Fedora – the forty-seventh and forty-eighth planets of the empire – 'for strategic reasons.' It was also hinted that Gooma, the sixty-second planet, might soon be given up also, 'in order to enable us to strengthen our positions else-where.'

So they were admitting something that could no longer be denied – namely, that two planets had gone down the drain, with a third soon to follow. Although they had not said so, it was pretty certain that what they had 'given up' the Terrans had captured. Mowry grinned to himself as words uttered in the cake shop came back to his mind.

'For months we have been making triumphant retreats before a demoralized enemy advancing in utter disorder.'

He went along the road and called the Café Susun. 'Did you collect?'

'We did,' said Skriva. 'And the next consignment is overdue.'

'I've read nothing about it.'

'You wouldn't – nothing having been written.'

'Well, I told you before that I pay when I've had proof. Until I get it, nothing doing. No proof, no dough.'

'We've got the evidence; it's up to you to take a look at it.'

Mowry thought swiftly. 'Still got the dyno handy?'

'Yar.'

'Maybe you'd better meet me. Make it the ten-time hour, same road, marker *den-8*.'

The car arrived on time. Mowry stood by the marker, a dim figure in the darkness of night with only fields and trees around. The car rolled up, headlights glaring. Skriva got out, took a small sack from the trunk, opened its top and exhibited its contents in the blaze of the lights.

'Lord!' Mowry gasped.

'It's a ragged job,' admitted Skriva. 'He had a tough neck, and Gurd was in a hurry. What's the matter?'

'I'm not complaining.'

'You bet you're not. Butin's the boy who's entitled to gripe.' Skriva kicked the sack. 'Aren't you, Butin?'

'Get rid of it,' ordered Mowry.

Skriva tossed the sack into an adjacent ditch, put out a hand. 'The money.'

Giving him the package, Mowry waited in silence while the other checked the contents inside the car with the help of Gurd. They thumbed the neat stack of notes lovingly, with much licking of lips and mutual congratulations.

When they had finished, Skriva chuckled. 'That was twenty thousand for nothing. We couldn't have got it easier.'

'What d'you mean, for nothing?'

'We'd have done it anyway, whether you'd named him or not. Butin was making ready to talk. You could see it in the slimy *soko's* eyes. What d'you say, Gurd?'

Gurd contented himself with a neck-wringing gesture.

'Nothing like being sure,' Mowry said. 'Now I've got another and different kind of job for you. Feel like taking it on?'

Without waiting for a response, he exhibited another package. 'In here are ten small gadgets. They're fitted with clips and have thin lengths of cable attached. I want these contraptions fastened to telephone lines in or near the centre of Pertane. They've got to be set in place so that they aren't visible from the street but so the cables can be seen hanging down.'

'But,' objected Skriva, 'if the cables can be seen, it's only a matter of time before somebody traces them up to the gadgets. Where's the sense of hiding what is sure to be found?'

'Where's the sense of me giving you good money to do it?' Mowry riposted.

'How much?'

'Five thousand guilders apiece. That's fifty thousand for the lot.'

Skriva pursed his lips in a silent whistle.

'I can check on whether you've actually fixed them,' Mowry continued, 'so don't try kidding me.'

Grabbing the package, Skriva said, 'I think you're crazy – but who am I to complain?'

Headlights brightened; the car set up a shrill whine and rocketed away. Mowry watched until it had gone from sight, then tramped back into Radine and made for the public booths. He phoned Kaitempi HQ, careful to keep his scanner switched off, and to give his voice the singsong tones of a native Jaimecan.

'Somebody's been decapitated.'

'*Hi?*'

'There's a head in a sack near marker *8-den* on the road to Pertane.'

'Who's that talking? Who . . .'

He cut off, leaving the voice to gargle futilely. They'd follow up the tip, no doubt of that. It was essential to his plans that authority should find the head and identify it. He went to his hotel, came out, mailed two hundred and twenty letters.

> Butin Urhava was the third.
> The list is long.
> Dirac Angestun Gesept.

That done, he enjoyed an hour's stroll before bedtime, pacing the streets and as usual pondering the day's work. It would not be long, he thought, before someone became curious about the hanging cables and an electrician, or telephone engineer, was called in to investigate. The inevitable result would be a hurried examination of Jaimec's entire telephone system and the discovery of several more taps.

Authority would then find itself confronted with three unanswerable questions, all of them ominous: who's been listening, for how long, and how much have they learned?

He did not envy those in precarious power, who were being subjected to this mock build-up of treachery, while elsewhere the allegedly defeated Terrans were taking over Sirian planets one after another. Uneasy lies the head that wears a crown – but infinitely more so when a wasp crawls into bed with it.

A little before the twelve-time hour, he turned into the road where his high-class hide-out was located and came to an abrupt halt. Outside the hotel stood a line of official cars, a fire pump and an ambulance. A number of uniformed cops were meandering around the vehicles. Tough-looking characters in plain clothes were all over the scene.

Two of the latter appeared out of nowhere and confronted him, hard-eyed.

'What's happened?' asked Mowry, imitating a Sunday-school superintendent.

'Never mind what's happened. Show us your documents. Come on, what are you waiting for?'

Carefully, James Mowry slid a hand into his inner pocket. They were tense, fully alert, watching his movement and ready to react if what he produced was not paper. He drew out his identity card and handed it over, knowing that it bore the proper cachet of Diracta and the overstamp of Jaimec. Then he gave them his personal card and movement permit. Inwardly he hoped with all his heart that they would be easily convinced.

They weren't; they displayed the dogged determination of those under strict orders to make someone pay dearly for something or other. Evidently whatever had occurred was serious enough to have stirred up a hornets' nest.

'A special correspondent,' said the larger of the two,

mouthing the words with contempt. He looked up from the identity card. 'What is special about a correspondent?'

'I've been sent here to cover the war news specifically from the Jaimec angle. I do not bother with civilian matters. Those are for ordinary reporters.'

'I see.' He gave Mowry a long, penetrating look. His eyes had the beady coldness of a sidewinder's. 'From where do you get your news about the war?'

'From official handouts – mostly from the Office of War Information in Pertane.'

'You have no other sources?'

'Yes, of course. I keep my ears open for rumours.'

'And what do you do with *that* stuff?'

'I try to draw reasonable conclusions from it, write it up and submit the script to the Board of Censorship. If they approve it, I'm lucky. If they kill it, well' – he spread his hands with an air of helplessness – 'I just put up with it.'

'Therefore,' said the Kaitempi agent cunningly, 'you should be well-known to officials of the Office of War Information and the Board of Censorship, *hi?* They will vouch for you if requested to do so, *hi?*'

'Without a doubt,' assented Mowry, praying for a break.

'Good! You will name the ones you know best, and we will check with them immediately.'

'What, at this time of night?'

'Why should you care what time it is? It is your neck . . .'

That did it. Mowry punched him on the snout, swiftly, fiercely, putting every ounce of weight behind the blow. The recipient went down good and hard, and stayed down.

The other fellow was no slouch; wasting no time in dumb-foundment, he took a bowlegged but quick step forward, shoved a gun into Mowry's face. 'Raise them high, you *soko*, or I'll . . .'

With the speed and recklessness of one who is desperate, Mowry ducked under the gun, seized the other's extended arm, got it over his shoulder and yanked. The agent let out a thin, piercing yelp and flew through the air with the greatest of ease. His gun dropped to the ground; Mowry scooped it up and started the sprint of his life.

Round the corner, along the street, and into an alley; this took him by the back of his hotel. As he tore past, he noted out the corner of one eye that a window was missing, and there was a great ragged hole in the wall. Hurdling a pile of smashed bricks and splintered timber, he reached the alley's end and shot across the next street.

So they had smelled him out, possibly through registration checks. They had searched his room and tried to open his bag with a metal master key. Then had come the big bang. If the room had been crowded at the time, the explosion would have enough force to kill at least a dozen of them.

Mowry kept going as fast as he could make it, the gun in his grip, his ears straining for sounds of pursuit. Pretty soon, the radio alarm would be going over the air; they'd close every exit from the town, blocking trains, buses, roads – everything. At all costs, he must beat them to it.

As far as possible, he kept to lanes and alleys, avoiding main roads on which patrol-cars would be running to and fro. At this late hour, there were no crowds in which to hide. The streets were almost empty, with most folk abed, and an armed man sprinting through the night was mighty conspicuous. But nothing could be done about that; to amble along with an air of innocence was to give time for the trap to close about him.

Darkness was his only help, not counting his legs. He pounded through alley after alley, bolted across six streets, halted in deep shadow as he was about to cross the seventh. A car bulging with cops and plain-clothes Kaitempi slid past, its windows full of faces trying to look everywhere at once.

For a short time, Mowry stood silent and unmoving in the shadow, heart thumping, chest heaving, a trickle of sweat creeping down his spine. As soon as the hunters had gone, he was across the street, into the opposite alley and racing onward.

Five times he paused in concealment, mentally cursing the delay, while prowl-cars snooped around.

The sixth stop was different. He lurked in the alley's corner as headlights came up the street. A mud-spattered dyno rolled into view and stopped within twenty yards of him. The next moment, a solitary civilian got out, went to a nearby door and shoved a key into its lock. James Mowry came out of the alley like a quick-moving cat.

The door opened just as the car shot away with a shrill scream from its dynamo. Struck with surprise, the civilian wasted half a minute gaping after his vanishing property. Then he let go an oath, ran indoors and snatched up the telephone.

Luck has to be mixed, decided Mowry, as he gripped the wheel; there must be good to compensate for bad. Swinging into a broad, well-lit avenue, he slowed to a more sedate pace.

Two overloaded patrol-cars passed him, going in the opposite direction; another overtook him and rocked ahead. They weren't interested in a dirty dyno; they were hunting a breathless fugitive assumed to be still afoot. He estimated that it would be another ten minutes before the radio made them change their minds. It might have been better if he had shot the car's owner; but he hadn't, and it was too late to regret the omission now.

After seven minutes he passed the last houses of Radine and headed into open country, along an unfamiliar road. At once he hit top speed; the car howled along, headlight beams dipping and swaying, the *den*-needle creeping close to its limit.

Twenty minutes later, he shot like a rocket through a village buried deep in slumber. One mile farther on he rounded a bend, got a brief glimpse of a white pole across the road, with the glitter of buttons and shine of metal helmets grouped at each end. He set his teeth, aimed straight at the middle without reducing speed. The car hit the pole, flung the broken halves aside, and raced on. Something struck five sharp blows on the back; two neat holes appeared in the rear window, and a third where the windshield joined the roof.

That showed the radio-alarm had been given; forces had been alerted over a wide area. His crashing of the roadblock was a giveaway. They now knew in which direction he was fleeing and could concentrate ahead of him. Just where he was going was more than Mowry knew himself. The locale was strange, and he had no map to consult. Worse, he had little money and no documents of any kind. The loss of his case had deprived him of everything except what was upon his person, plus a hot car and a stolen gun.

Soon he reached a crossroad with a marker dimly visible on each corner. Braking violently, he jumped out and peered at the nearest one in the poor light of night. It said *Radine – 27 den.* The opposite marker said *Valapan – 92 den.* So that's where he'd been heading – to Valapan. Doubtless the police there were out in full strength.

The marker on the left-hand road read *Pertane – 51 den.* He clambered back into the car and turned left. There were no signs of close pursuit, but that meant nothing. Somebody with radio contact and a big map would be moving cars around to head him off as reports of his position filtered in.

At the marker indicating *9 den* he found another crossroad which he recognized. The sky-glow of Pertane now shone straight ahead, while on his right was the road leading to the cave in the forest. He took an added risk of interception by driving the car a couple of miles nearer Pertane before abandoning it. When they found it there, they'd probably jump to the conclusion that he'd sought refuge somewhere in the big city; it would be all to the good if they wasted time and man power scouring Pertane from end to end.

Walking back, he reached the forest and continued along its fringe. It took him two hours to arrive at the tree and the tombstone. During that period he dived into the woods eleven times, and watched carloads of hunters whine past. It looked as if he'd drawn a veritable army into chasing around in the night; that was a worthwhile result, if Wolf was to be believed.

Entering the forest, he made for the cave.

*

At the cave, Mowry found everything intact and undisturbed. He arrived thankfully, feeling that he was as safe here as he could be anywhere upon a hostile world. It was hardly likely that the hunt would succeed in tracking him through twenty miles of virgin forest, even if it occurred to them to try.

For a short time he sat on a container and let his mind indulge a wrestling match between duty and desire. Orders were that on each visit to the cave he must use the transmitter and send an up-to-the-minute report. There was no need to guess what might happen if he were to do so this time; they'd order him to stay put and indulge in no further activities. Later, they'd send a ship, pick him up, and deposit him on some other Sirian planet where he could start all over again. They'd leave his successor on Jaimec.

The thought riled him; it was all very well for them to talk about the tactical advantages of replacing a known operator with an unknown one; but to the man who suffered replacement, it smacked of incompetence and defeat. James Mowry flatly refused to consider himself either inefficient or beaten.

Besides, he had carried out phase one and part of phase two. There was still phase three, the build-up of pressure to the point where the foe would be so busy defending the back door that he'd be in no condition to hold the front one.

Phase three involved strategic bombing, both by Mowry himself, and by anyone he could pay to do it. He had the necessary material for the former and the money for the latter. In yet unopened containers lay enough money to buy a dozen battleships and give every man of their crews a large box of cigars. There were forty different kinds of infernal machines, not one of them recognizable for what it was, and all guaranteed to go *whump* in the right place, at the right moment.

He was not supposed to start offensive action of the phase-three type until ordered to do so, because usually it preceded full-scale attack by Terran space-forces. But in the meantime he could work his way up to it by keeping *Dirac Angestun Gesept* in the public eye.

No, he would not signal just yet; he would play around a bit longer – long enough to establish his right to remain to the bitter end, regardless of whether the Kaitempi had him taped. He'd been run out of Radine, but he wasn't going to be chased right off the planet!

Opening a couple of containers, Mowry undressed and put on a wide belt that made him corpulent with guilders. Then he donned ill-cut, heavy clothes typical of the Sirian farmer. A couple of cheek-pads widened and rounded his face. He plucked his eyebrows into slight raggedness and trimmed his hair to comply with the current agricultural fashion.

With purple dye he gave his face the peculiar mottling of a bad complexion. The final touch was to give himself an injection alongside his right nostril; within two hours, it would create that faint orange-coloured blemish occasionally seen on Sirian features.

He was now a middle-aged, coarse-looking, and somewhat overfed Sirian farmer. This time he was Rathan Gusulkin, a grain grower; his papers showed that he had emigrated from Diracta five years ago. This explained his Mashambi accent, the one thing he could not conceal.

Before setting out in his new rôle, he enjoyed another genuine Earth-meal and four hours of much-needed sleep. When two miles from the outskirts of Pertane, he buried a package holding fifty thousand guilders at the base of the southernmost left-hand buttress of the bridge across the river. Not far from the point, beneath deep water, a typewriter lay in the mud.

From the first booth in Pertane he called the Café Susun. The answer was prompt, the voice strange and curt, and the distant scanner was not operating.

'That the Café Susun?' Mowry asked.

'Yar.'

'Skriva there?'

A brief silence, followed by, 'He's somewhere around. Upstairs or out back. Who wants him?'

'His mother.'

'Don't give me that!' rasped the voice. 'I can tell by your . . .'

'What's it got to do with you?' Mowry shouted. 'Is Skriva there or not?'

The voice became suddenly subdued and sounded completely out of character as it cajoled, 'Hold on a moment. I'll go find him for you.'

'You needn't bother. Is Gurd there?'

'No, he hasn't been in today. Hold on, I tell you. I'll go find Skriva. He's upstairs or . . .'

'Listen!' ordered Mowry. He stuck his tongue between his lips and blew hard.

Then he dropped the phone, scrambled out the booth and hightailed it at the fastest pace that would not attract attention. Nearby, a bored shopkeeper lounged in his doorway and idly watched him go; so did four people gossiping outside the shop. That meant five witnesses, five descriptions of the fellow who had just used the booth.

'Hold on!' the strange voice had urged. It wasn't the voice of the barkeep, or the careless, slangy tones of any frequenter of the Café Susun. It had the characteristic bossiness of a plain-clothes cop or a Kaitempi agent. Yar, hold on, Stupid, while we trace the call and pick you up.

Three hundred yards along the road, Mowry jumped on a bus. Looking backward, he could not tell whether the shopkeeper and the gossips had noticed what he had done. The bus lumbered on. A police car rocked past it and braked by the booth. The bus turned a corner, and Mowry wondered just how close a close shave can be.

The Café Susun was staked out, no doubt of that; the cops' prompt arrival at the booth proved it. How they had obtained a line on the place, and what had induced them to raid it, was a matter of sheer speculation. Perhaps they'd been led to it by their investigations of the late Butin Urhava.

Or perhaps Gurd and Skriva had been nabbed while tramping heavy-footed all over a roof and waving cables across a street. If they had been caught, they'd talk, tough as they were. When fingernails are pulled out, one by one, or when intermittent voltage from a battery is applied to the corners of the eyeballs, the most granite-hard character becomes positively garrulous.

Yes, they'd talk – but all they could tell was a weird tale about a crackpot with a Mashambi accent and an inexhaustible supply of guilders. Not a word about *Dirac Angestun Gesept*; not a syllable about Terran intervention on Jaimec.

But there were others who'd talk to better effect.

'You see anyone leave this booth just now?'

'Yar. A fat yokel. Seemed in a hurry.'

'Where'd he go?'

'Down the road. Got on a forty-two bus.'

'What did he look like? Describe him as accurately as you can. Come on, be quick about it!'

'Medium height, middle-aged, round-faced, got a bad complexion. Quite a belly on him, too. Had a red *falkin* alongside his nose. Wearing a fur jacket, brown cord pants, heavy brown boots. Looked the farmer type.'

'That's enough for us. Jalek, let's get after that bus. Where's the mike – I'd better broadcast this description. We'll nail him if we move fast.'

'He's a cunning one. Didn't take him long to smell a trap when Lathin answered his call. He blew a vulgar noise and ran. Bet you the bus-jump is a blind – he's got a car parked somewhere.'

'Save your breath and catch up with that bus. Two of them have escaped us already. We'll have a lot of explaining to do if we lose a third.'

'Yar, I know.'

NINE

Mowry got off the bus before anyone had time to overtake it, and caught another one running on a transverse route. But he did not play tag all over the city as before. The pursuers almost certainly had a description of him and it looked as if he had most of Jaimec on the jump.

His third change put him on an express bus heading out of town. It dropped him a mile beyond the bridge where he had hidden fifty thousand guilders. Once again he was heading back to the forest and the cave.

To retrace his steps to the bridge and try to unearth the money would be dangerous. Police cars would be heading this way before long; the hunt for a potbellied farmer would not be confined to Pertane. So long as daylight remained, the best thing for James Mowry to do was to get out of sight and stay out until he could assume yet another new guise.

Moving fast, he reached the edge of the forest without being stopped and questioned. For a short time he continued to use the road, seeking shelter among the trees whenever a car approached. But traffic increased and vehicles appeared with such frequency that eventually he gave up hope of further progress before dark. He was pretty tired, too; his eyelids were heavy and his feet had taken a beating.

Penetrating farther into the woods he found a comfortable, well-concealed spot; he lay on a thick bed of moss and let go a sigh of satisfaction.

Wolf had asserted that one man could pin down an army.

Mowry wondered how large a number he'd fastened and what real good it had done, if any. How many precious man-hours had his presence cost the foe? Thousands, tens of thousands, millions? To what forms of war service would those man-hours have been devoted if James Mowry had not compelled the enemy to waste them in other directions? Ah, in the answer to that hypothetical question lay the true measure of a wasp's efficiency.

Gradually he gave up these unprofitable musings and drifted into sleep. Night was upon him when he awoke, refreshed, energetic, and feeling less bitter at events. Things could have been worse, much worse. For example, he could have gone straight to the Café Susun and walked into the arms of the Kaitempi. They'd hold him on general principles, and he doubted his ability to hold out once they really got to work on him. About the only captives from whom the Kaitempi had extracted nothing were those who had managed to commit suicide before questioning.

As he trudged steadily through the dark toward the cave, he blessed his luck, wisdom, or intuition in making a phone call. Then his thoughts became occupied with Gurd and Skriva. If they had been caught, it meant he'd been deprived of valuable allies and once again was strictly on his own. But if, like himself, they had escaped the trap, how was he going to find them?

Arriving at the cave as dawn was breaking, Mowry took off his shoes, sat on the pebble beach, and soaked his aching feet in the stream. Still his mind chewed unceasingly at the question of how to find Gurd and Skriva, if they were still free. Eventually, the Kaitempi would remove the stakeout from the Café Susun – either because they were satisfied that they had exploited it to the limit, or because of pressure of other business. It would then be possible to visit the place and find someone able to give all the information he needed. But heaven alone knew when that would be.

In new and radically changed disguise, he could loll around the neighbourhood of the café until he found one of its regular customers and use him as a lead to Gurd and Skriva. But the chances were high that the Café Susun was the focal point of Kaitempi activity over the entire district, with plain-clothes men keeping watch for suspicious-looking characters anywhere within a mile of the place.

After an hour's meditation, Mowry decided that there was one possibility of regaining contact with the brothers. It depended not only on their being on the loose, but also having their fair share of brains and imagination. It might work; they were crude and ruthless, but not stupid.

He could leave them a message where he'd left one before, on the Radine road under marker *33 den*. If they had successfully completed their last job, they had fifty thousand guilders coming to them; that should be more than enough to sharpen their wits.

The sun came up, spreading its warmth through the trees and into the cave. It was one of those days that beguiles a man into lying around and doing nothing. Succumbing to temptation, Mowry gave himself a holiday and postponed further action until the morrow. It was just as well; constant chasing around, uneasy sleep, and much nervous tension had combined to thin him down and tax his resources.

All that day he loafed in or near the cave, enjoying peace and stillness, cooking himself large and succulent Earth-meals.

Evidently the enemy was obsessed with the notion that the quarry sought sanctuary only in heavily populated places; it just hadn't occurred to them that anyone would take to the wilds. This was logical enough from their viewpoint, they having accepted *Dirac Angestun Gesept* as a large, well-organized group, too big and widespread to lurk in a cave. The wasp had magnified himself to such proportions that they weren't going to waste time looking in holes for him.

That night, James Mowry slept like a child, soundly and solidly, right around the clock. He spent the next morning in total idleness, had a bath in the stream during the heat of noon. Toward evening, he cropped his hair in military fashion, leaving himself with no more than a stiff bristle covering his skull.

Another injection obliterated the *falkin*. He retinted himself all over, making his colour a fresher and slightly deeper purple. Dental plates filled the gaps where his wisdom teeth had been, and made his face appear wider, heavier, and with squarer jawline.

A complete change of clothing followed. The shoes he donned were of military type; the civilian suit was of expensive cut; the neck-scarf was knotted in space-marine fashion. To this ensemble he added a platinum watch fob and a platinum wristband holding an ornamental identity disc.

He now looked like somebody several cuts above the Sirian average. The new set of documents he pocketed confirmed this impression. They vouched for the fact that he was Colonel Krasna Halopti of the Military Intelligence Service, and as such entitled to claim the assistance of all Sirian authorities any time, anywhere.

Satisfied that he now looked the part one hundred per cent, and bore little resemblance to any of his previous manifestations, Mowry sat on a container and wrote a brief letter.

'I tried to get in touch with you at the café and found the place full of *K-sokos*. The money had been buried in readiness for you at the base of the southernmost left-hand buttress of the Asako Bridge. If you are free, and if you are able and willing to take on more work, leave a message here saying when and where I can find you.'

Leaving it unsigned, he folded it and slipped it into a damp-proof cellophane envelope. Into his pocket he dropped a small, silent automatic. The gun was of Sirian manufacture and he had a forged permit to carry it.

This new role was more daring and dangerous than the others had been; a check with official records would expose and damn him in double-quick time. But it had its compensations in the average Sirian's respect for authority. Provided that he conducted himself with enough self-assurance and sufficient arrogance, even the Kaitempi might be tempted to accept him now at face value.

Two hours after the fall of darkness he switched Container-22 and set forth through the forest, bearing a new case larger and heavier than before. Again he found himself regretting the distance of his hide-out from the nearest road; a twenty-mile march each way was tedious and tiring. But it was a small price to pay for the security of his supplies.

The walk was longer this time because he did not cut straight through to the road and thumb a lift. In his new guise, this would be out of character, and draw unwelcome attention. So he followed the fringe of the forest to the point where two other roads joined on. Here, in the early morning, he waited between the trees until an express bus appeared in the distance. He stepped out onto the road, caught it and was carried into the centre of Pertane.

Within half an hour, he found a parked dyno that suited his purpose, got in, and drove away. Nobody ran after him yelling bloody murder; the theft had gone unobserved.

At the Radine road, he stopped, waited for the artery to clear in both directions, and buried his letter under the marker. Then he returned to Pertane and put the car back where he had found it. He had been away a little over an hour and it was probable that the owner had not missed the machine.

Next, Mowry went to the crowded main post office, took half a dozen small but heavy parcels from his case, addressed them and mailed them. Each held an airtight can containing a cheap clock-movement and a piece of paper, nothing else. The clock-movement emitted a sinister tick – just loud enough to be heard if a suspicious-minded person listened closely. The paper bore a message short and to the point.

> *This package could have killed you.*
> *Two different packages brought together at the right time and place could kill a hundred thousand.*
> *End this war before we end you!*
> *Dirac Angestun Gesept.*

Paper threats, that was all – but they were effective enough to eat still further into the enemy's war effort. They'd alarm the recipients and give their forces something more to worry about. Doubtless the military would provide a personal bodyguard for every big wheel on Jaimec; that alone would pin down a regiment.

Mail would be examined, and all suspicious parcels would be taken apart in a blast-proof room. There'd be a city-wide search with radiation-detectors for the component parts of a fission bomb. Civil defence would be alerted in readiness to cope with a mammoth explosion that might or might not take place. Anyone on the streets who walked with a secretive air and wore a slightly mad expression would be arrested and hauled in for questioning.

Yes, after three murders, with the promise of more to come, authority dare not dismiss *DAG*'s threats as the idle talk of some crackpot on the loose.

As Mowry strolled along the road he amused himself by picturing the scene when the receiver of a parcel rushed to dump it in a bucket of water while someone else frantically phoned for the bomb squad. He was so engrossed with these thoughts that it was some time before he became conscious of a shrill whistling sound rising and falling over Pertane. He stopped, looked around, gazed at the sky, but saw nothing out of the ordinary. Most people seemed to have disappeared from the street; but a few, like himself, were standing and staring around bewilderedly.

The next moment a cop shoved him in the shoulder. 'Get down, you fool!'

'Down?' Mowry eyed him without understanding. 'Down where? What's the matter?'

'Into the cellars,' shouted the cop, making shooing motions. 'Don't you recognize a raid-alarm when you hear it?' Without waiting for a reply, he ran forward bawling at other people, 'Get down! Get down!'

Turning, Mowry scrambled after the others down a long

steep flight of steps and into the basement of a business block. He was surprised to find the place already crowded. Several hundred people had taken refuge without having to be told. They were standing around, or sitting on wooden benches, or leaning against the wall. Upending his case, Mowry sat on it.

Nearby an irate oldster looked him over with rheumy gaze and said, 'A raid-alarm. What d'you think of that?'

'Nothing,' answered Mowry, 'What's the use of thinking? There's nothing we can do about it.'

'But the Spakum fleets have been destroyed,' shrilled the oldster, making James Mowry the focal point of an address to everyone. 'They've said so time and again, on the radio and in the papers. The Spakum fleets have been wiped out. So what has set off an alarm, *hi?* What can raid us, *hi?* Tell me that!'

'Maybe it's just a practice alarm,' Mowry soothed.

'Practice?' He spluttered with senile fury. 'Why do we need practice and who says so? If the Spakum forces are beaten, we've no need to hide. There's nothing to hide from!'

'Don't pick on me,' advised Mowry, bored with the other's whines. 'I didn't sound the alarm.'

'Some stinking idiot sounded it,' persisted the oldster. 'Some lying *soko* who wants us to believe the war is as good as over when it isn't. How do we know how much truth there is in what they're telling us?' He spat on the floor. 'A great victory in the Centauri sector – then the raid-alarm is sounded. They must think we're a lot of . . .'

A squat, heavily built character stepped close to the speaker and snapped, 'Shut up!'

The oldster was too absorbed in his woes to cower, too pigheaded to recognize the voice of authority. 'I won't shut up. I am walking home when somebody pushed me down here just because a whistle blows and . . .'

The squat man opened his jacket, displayed a badge, and repeated in harsher tones, 'I said shut up!'

'Who d'you think you are? At my time of life I'm not going to be . . .'

With a swift movement, the squat man whipped out a rubber truncheon and larruped the oldster over the head. The victim went down like a shot steer.

A voice at the back of the crowd shouted, 'Shame!' Several others murmured, fidgeted, but did nothing.

Grinning, the squat man showed what he thought of this disapproval by kicking the victim repeatedly. Glancing up, he met Mowry's gaze and promptly challenged, 'Well?'

Mowry said evenly, 'Are you of the Kaitempi?'

'Yar. What's it to you?'

'Nothing. I was only curious.'

'Then don't be. Keep your dirty nose out of this.'

The crowd muttered and fidgeted again. Two cops came down from the street, sat on the bottom step and mopped their foreheads. They looked nervous and jumpy. The Kaitempi agent joined them, took a gun out of his pocket and nursed it in his lap. Mowry smiled at him enigmatically.

Now the silence of the city crept into the cellar. The crowd became peculiarly tense as everyone listened. After half an hour, a series of hisses were heard. They started on a loud, strong note and swiftly faded into the sky.

Tenseness increased with the knowledge that guided missiles weren't being expended for the fun of it. Somewhere overhead, within theoretical range, must be a Spakum ship – perhaps bearing a load that might drop at any moment.

There was another volley of hisses; then the silence returned. The cops and the agent got to their feet, edged farther into the basement, and turned to watch the steps. Individual breathing could be heard, some respirating spasmodically as if finding difficulty in using their lungs. All faces betrayed an inward strain and there was an acrid smell of sweat. Mowry's only thought was that to be disintegrated in a bomb-blast from his own side was a hell of a way to die.

Ten minutes later the floor quivered; the walls vibrated; the entire building shook. From the street came the brittle crash of breaking glass as windows fell out. Still there was no other sound, no roar of a great explosion, no dull rumbling of propulsors in the stratosphere. The quietness was eerie in the extreme.

It was three hours before the same whistling on a lower note proclaimed the all-clear. The crowd hurried out, vastly relieved. They stepped over the oldster, left him lying there. The two cops headed together up the street while the Kaitempi agent strode the opposite way.

Mowry caught up with the agent and spoke pleasantly. 'Shock damage only. They must have dropped it a good distance away.'

The other grunted.

'I wanted to speak to you, but couldn't very well do so in front of all those people.'

'Yar? Why not?'

For answer, James Mowry produced his identity card and his warrant.

'Colonel Halopti, Military Intelligence.' Returning the card, the agent lost some of his belligerence and made an effort to be polite. 'What did you want to say – something about the garrulous old fool?'

'No. He deserved all he got. You're to be commended for the way you handled him.' He noted the other's look of gratification and added, 'An ancient gab like him could have made the whole crowd hysterical.'

'Yar, that's right. The way to control a mob is to cut out and beat up its spokesman.'

'When the alarm sounded, I was on my way to Kaitempi HQ to borrow a dependable agent,' explained Mowry. 'When I saw you in action I felt you'd save me the trouble. You're just the fellow I want: one who's quick on the uptake and will stand no nonsense. What's your name?'

'Sagramatholou.'

'Ah, you're from the K17 system, *hi?* They all use compound names there, don't they?'

'Yar. And you're from Diracta. Halopti is a Driactan name, and you've got a Mashambi accent.'

Mowry laughed. 'Can't hide much from each other, can we?'

'Nar,' He looked Mowry over with open curiosity. 'What d'you want me for?'

'I hope to nab the leader of a *DAG* cell. It's got to be done quickly and quietly. If the Kaitempi put fifty on the job and make a major operation of it, they'll scare away the rest for miles around. One at a time is the best technique. As the Spakums say, "*Softly, softly, catchee monkey.*" '

'Yar, that's the best way,' agreed Sagramatholou.

'I'm confident that I could take this character single-handed, without frightening away the others. But while I'm going in at the front he may beat it out the back, so it needs two of us. I want a reliable man to grab him if he bolts. You'll get full credit for the capture.'

The other's eyes narrowed and gained an eager light. 'I'll be glad to come along if it's all right with HQ. I'd better phone and ask them.'

'Please yourself,' said Mowry with a carelessness he was far from feeling. 'But you know what will happen for sure.'

'What d'you think?'

'They'll take you off it and give me an officer of equivalent rank.' Mowry made a disparaging gesture. 'Although I shouldn't say it, being a colonel myself, I'd rather have a tough, experienced man of my own choice.'

The other swelled his chest. 'You may have something. There are officers and officers.'

'Precisely! Well, are you in this with me or not?'

'Do you accept full responsibility if my superiors gripe about it?'

'Of course.'

'That's good enough for me. When do we start?'

'At once.'

'All right,' said Sagramatholou, making up his mind. 'I'm on duty another three hours anyway.'

'Good! You got a civilian-type dyno?'

'All our dynos are ordinary-looking ones.'

'Mine bears military insignia,' lied Mowry. 'We'd better use yours.'

The other accepted this statement without question; he was completely hooked by his own eagerness to get credit for an important capture, and the prospect of finding another victim for the strangling-post.

Reaching the car-park around the corner, Sagramatholou took his seat behind the wheel of a big black dyno. Tossing his case into the back, Mowry got in beside him. The car edged onto the street.

'Where to?'

'South end, back of the Rida Engine Plant. I'll show you from there.'

Theatrically, the agent made a chopping motion with one hand as he said, 'This *DAG* business is sending us crazy. High time we put an end to it. How did you get a lead on them?'

'We picked it up on Diracta. One of them fell into our hands and talked.'

'In great pain?' suggested Sagramatholou, chuckling.

'Yar.'

'That's the way to handle them. They all blab when it's too much to endure. Then they die just the same.'

'Yar,' repeated James Mowry, with becoming gusto.

'We snatched a dozen from a café in the Laksin quarter,' continued Sagramatholou. 'They're talking, too. But they aren't talking sense – yet. They've admitted every crime in the calendar except membership of *DAG*. About that organization they know nothing, so they say.'

'What took you to the café?'

'Somebody got his stupid head lopped off. He was a regular frequenter of the joint. We identified him after a lot of trouble, traced him back and grabbed a bunch of his ever-loving friends. About six of them have confessed to the killing.'

'Six?' Mowry frowned.

'Yar. They did it at six different times, in six different places, for six different reasons. The dirty *sokos* are lying to make us ease up. But we'll get the truth yet.'

'Sounds like a mere hoodlum squabble to me. Where's the political angle, if any?'

'I don't know. The higher-ups keep things to themselves. They say they know for a fact that it was a *DAG* execution, and therefore whoever did it is a *DAG* killer.'

'Maybe somebody tipped them,' offered Mowry.

'Maybe somebody did. And he could be a liar, too.' Sagramatholou snorted. 'This war is enough without traitors and liars making things worse. We're being ran ragged, see? It can't go on forever.'

'Any luck with the snap searches?'

'There was at first. Then the luck petered out because everyone became wary. We've stopped making them for ten days. The lull will give the dodgers a sense of false security. When they're ripe for the taking, we'll take them.'

'That's good. One has to use one's wits these days, *hi?*'

'Yar.'

'Here we are. Turn left and then first right.'

The car shot past the rear of the engine plant, entered a narrow, rutted road, then switched into another, little better than a lane. All around was an unsavoury, semi-deserted area of old buildings, vacant lots and garbage dumps. They stopped and got out.

Gazing about him, the Kaitempi agent remarked, 'A typical vermin-run. Where now?'

'Along this alley.'

Mowry led the way into the alley, which was long, dirty, and had a dead end. They reached a twelve-foot wall that blocked further progress. There was nobody in sight; nothing could be heard save a distant hum of traffic and the nearer squeak of a hanging sign, old and rusty.

Pointing to the door set in the wall, Mowry said, 'This is the bolt-hole. It will take me two or three minutes to get round the front and go in. After that, you can expect anything.' He tried the door; it refused to budge. 'Locked.'

'Better unlock it so he can make a clear run,' suggested Sagramatholou. 'If he finds himself balked, he's liable to try to shoot it out with you and I'll be in no position to take part. These *sokos* can become dangerous when desperate.' He felt in a pocket, produced a bunch of master keys and grinned. 'The easiest way is to let him rush straight into my arms.' With that, he faced the door, turning his back on Mowry while he meddled with the lock. Mowry looked back along the alley. Still nobody in sight.

Taking out his gun, Mowry said in calm, unhurried tones, 'You kicked the old geezer when he was down.'

'Sure did,' agreed the agent, still trying the lock. 'I hope he dies slowly, the half-witted . . .' His voice broke off as the incongruity of Mowry's remark sank into his mind. He turned round, one hand braced upon the door, and looked straight into the gun's muzzle. 'What's this? What are you . . .'

'*Dirac Angestun Gesept,*' said Mowry. The gun in the hand emitted a *phut*, no louder than that of an air pistol. Sagramatholou remained standing, a blue hole in his forehead. His mouth hung open in an idiotic gape. Then his knees gave way and he plunged forward face first.

Pocketing the gun, James Mowry bent over the body. Working fast, he searched it, replaced the wallet after a swift look through it, but confiscated the official badge. Hastening out of the alley, he got into the car, drove it downtown to within a short distance of a used-car lot.

Walking the rest of the way, he looked over the big assembly of badly beaten-up dynos. A thin, hard-faced Sirian sidled up to him, noting Mowry's well-cut suit, his platinum fob and wristband.

'Lucky you!' announced the Sirian greasily. 'You have found the best place on Jaimec for a genuine bargain. Every car a real sacrifice. There's a war on, prices are going to jump and you just can't go wrong. Now take a look at this beauty right here. A gift, a positive gift. It's a . . .'

'I've got eyes,' said Mowry.

'Yar, sure. I'm pointing out . . .'

'I've got a mind of my own,' Mowry informed him. 'And I wouldn't drive around in any of these relics unless I was in a hurry to be struck dead.'

'But . . .'

'Like everyone else, I know there's a war on. Before long it's going to be mighty tough getting bits and pieces. I'm interested in something I can strip down for parts.' He pointed. 'That one, for instance. How much?'

'She's a good runner,' expostulated the salesman, donning a look of horror. 'Purrs along like brand new. Got current plates . . .'

'I can see it's got current plates.'

'. . . and is good and solid from front to back. I'm giving it away, just *giving* it.'

'How much?'

'Nine-ninety,' said the other, again eyeing the suit and the platinum.

'Robbery,' declared Mowry.

They haggled until Mowry got it for eight-twenty, in counterfeit money. He paid and drove it away. It creaked, groaned, and lurched in a manner that showed he'd been soaked for at least two hundred, but he wasn't resentful.

On a lot littered with scrap iron a mile away, with nobody watching, he parked the car, smashed its windshield and lamps, removed its wheels and number plates, took all detachable parts from the motor and effectively converted the machine into what any passer-by could see was an abandoned wreck. He walked off and returned shortly with the late Sagramatholou's car and loaded the loose parts into it.

Half an hour later, he slung the wheels and other items into the river; with them went Sagramatholou's plates. He drove away bearing the plates taken from the wreck; a police patrol or another Kaitempi car could now follow him for miles without spotting the number for which undoubtedly they'd be seeking.

Assured of no more snap searches for the time being, he idled around town until dark. Dumping the car in an underground garage, he bought a paper and perused it during a meal.

According to this newspaper, a lone Terran destroyer – 'a cowardly sneak-raider' – had managed to make a desperate dash through formidable space defences and drop one bomb upon the great national armaments complex at Shugruma. Little damage had been done. The invader had been blown apart soon afterward.

The story had been written up to give the impression that a sly dog had got in a harmless bite and been shot for its pains. Mowry wondered how many readers believed it. Shugruma was more than three hundred miles away – yet Pertane had shuddered to the shock-waves of the distant explosion. If that was anything to go by, the target area must now be represented by a crater a couple of miles in diameter.

The second page stated that forty-eight members of the traitorous Sirian Freedom Party had been seized by forces of law and order and would be dealt with appropriately. No details offered, no names given, no charges stated.

The forty-eight were doomed, whoever they were, or whoever they were thought to be. Alternatively, the whole yarn could be an officially concocted lie. The powers that be were quite capable of venting their fury on half a dozen common crooks and, for public consumption, defining them as *DAG* members while multiplying their number by eight.

One of the back pages devoted a few lines to the modest statement that Sirian forces had now been withdrawn from the planet Gooma 'so that they can be deployed more effectively in the actual area of combat.' This implied that Gooma was far outside the area of combat, a transparent piece of nonsense to any reader capable of independent thought. But ninety per cent of the readership could not endure the awful strain of thinking.

Far and away the most significant item was the leader-writer's contribution. This was a pompous sermon based on the thesis that total war should end only in total victory, which could and must be gained only by total effort. There was no room for political division within the Sirian ranks. Everyone without exception must be solidly behind the leadership in its determination to fight the war to a successful conclusion. Doubters and waverers, dodgers and complainers, the lazy and the shiftless were as much traitors to the cause as any spy or saboteur. They should be dealt with swiftly, once and for all.

Clearly, this was a yelp of agony, although *Dirac Angestun Gesept* was not mentioned in plain words. Since all such lectures were officially inspired, it was reasonable to assume that the brass hats were experiencing acute pain; in effect, they were shouting out loud that a wasp could sting. Perhaps some of them had received little parcels that ticked, and did not approve of this switch from the general to the personal.

Now that night had fallen, James Mowry took his case to his room. He made the approach warily. Any hide-out could become a trap at any time, without warning. Apart from the possibility of the police or Kaitempi lying in wait after having obtained a line on him, there was also the chance of encountering a landlord who'd become curious about the use of the room by another and more prosperous-looking character.

The building wasn't watched; the room was not staked out. Mowry managed to sneak in unobserved. Everything proved to be exactly as he had left it, showing that no one had found reason to come nosing around. Thankfully he sprawled on the bed and gave his feet a rest while he considered the situation. It was evident that, as far as possible, he would have to enter and leave the room only during hours of darkness. The alternative was to seek another hide-out, preferably in an area more in keeping with his present character.

The following day he regretted the destruction of his first case and all its contents in Radine. This loss piled up the work, but it had to be done. As a result he spent all morning in the public library compiling a list of names and addresses to replace the previous one. Then with plain paper, envelopes and a small hand-printer he used another two days preparing a stack of letters. It was a relief when they were finished and mailed.

Sagramatholou was the fourth.
The list is long.
Dirac Angestun Gesept.

Thus he had killed several birds with one stone. He had avenged the oldster – an act that gave him a good deal of satisfaction; he had struck another blow at the Kaitempi, and he had acquired a car not traceable through renting agencies or usual sales channels. Finally he had given the authorities further proof of *DAG*'s willingness to kill, maim, or otherwise muscle its way to power.

To boost this situation, he mailed another six parcels at the same time. Outwardly these were identical with the former ones; they emitted the same subdued tick. There the resemblance ended. At periods varying between six and twenty hours after sending, or at any moment that someone tried to pry them open, they were due to go off with a bang sufficiently forceful to plaster a body against the wall.

On the fourth day after his return to the room he slipped out unseen, collected the car and visited marker *33-den* on the Radine road. Several patrol-cars passed him on the way, but none betrayed the slightest interest in him. Reaching the marker, he dug at its base, found his own cellophane envelope, now containing a small card. All it said was *Asako 19–1713*.

The trick had come off.

TEN

Forthwith Mowry drove back to the first booth he could find, switched off its scanner, and called the number. A strange voice answered while the visi-screen remained blank. Evidently there was similar caution at the other end.

'19–1713,' it said.

'Gurd or Skriva there?' asked Mowry.

'Wait,' ordered the voice.

'One moment and no more,' retorted Mowry. 'After that – goodbye!'

The only answer was a grunt. Mowry hung on, watching the road, ready to drop the phone and depart the instant his intuition told him to get away fast.

He was nearing the point of taking alarm when Skriva's voice came through and growled, 'Who's that?'

'Your benefactor.'

'Oh, you. I'm not getting your pic.'

'I'm not getting yours, either.'

'This is no place to talk,' said Skriva. 'We'd better meet. Where are you?'

A swift series of thoughts flashed through Mowry's mind. *Where are you?* Was Skriva allowing himself to be used as bait? If he'd been caught and given a preliminary taste of rough treatment, this was just the sort of crafty trick the Kaitempi would play.

On the other hand, it wasn't likely in such circumstances that Skriva would bother asking for Mowry's location; the Kaitempi would know it already, having traced the call. Moreover they'd want the conversation prolonged as much as possible, to hold their quarry on the spot. Skriva was trying to cut it short; yes, the odds were against a trap.

'You struck dumb?' shouted Skriva, impatient and suspicious.

'I was thinking. How about meeting me where you left your phone number?'

'That's as good as anywhere.'

'By yourself,' warned Mowry, 'Nobody else with you except Gurd. Nobody following and nobody hanging around.'

Driving back to the marker, James Mowry parked his car on the verge and waited. Twenty minutes afterward, Skriva's dyno rolled up, parked behind. Skriva got out, approached him, halted in mid-step, scowled uncertainly, slid a hand into a pocket and looked hurriedly up and down the road. There were no other ears in sight.

Mowry grinned at him. 'What's eating you? Got a guilty conscience or something?'

Coming closer, Skriva eyed him with slight incredulity, then commented, 'So it *is* you. What have you been doing to yourself?' Without waiting for a reply, he walked around the hood, climbed in, took the other seat. 'You don't look the same. It was hard to recognize you.'

'That's the idea. A change for the better wouldn't do you any harm, either. Make it harder for the cops to get you.'

'Maybe.' Skriva was silent for a moment. 'They got Gurd.'

Mowry sat up, 'How? When was this?'

'The damn fool came down from a roof straight into the arms of two of them. Not satisfied with that, he gave them some lip and went for his gun.'

'If he'd behaved as if he'd every right to be up there, he could have talked his way out of it.'

'Gurd couldn't talk his way out of an old sack,' opined Skriva. 'He's not made like that. I've spent a lot of time keeping him out of trouble.'

'How come you weren't collared too?'

'I was on another roof halfway down the street. They didn't see me. It was all over before I could get down.'

'What happened to him?'

'What you'd expect. The cops were already beating him over the head before he got his hand in his pocket. Last I saw of him was when they threw him into the wagon.'

'Tough luck!' sympathized Mowry. He meditated a while, and asked, 'And what happened at the Café Susun?'

'Don't know for sure. Gurd and I weren't there at the time, and a fellow tipped us to stay clear. All I know is that the Kaitempi rushed the place twenty strong, grabbed everyone in sight and staked it. I've not shown my face near there since. Some *soko* must have talked too much.'

'Butin Urhava, for instance?'

'How could he?' scoffed Skirva. 'Gurd finished him off before he had a chance to blab.'

'Maybe he talked *after* Gurd had tended to him,' Mowry suggested. 'Sort of lost his head about it.'

Skriva narrowed his eyes. 'What d'you mean?'

'Oh, forget it. Did you collect that roll from the bridge?'

'Yar.'

'Want any more – or are you now too rich to care?'

Studying him calculatingly, Skriva asked, 'How much money have you got together?'

'Enough to pay for all the jobs I want done.'

'That tells me nothing.'

'It isn't intended to,' Mowry assured him. 'What's on your mind?'

'I like money.'

'That fact is more than apparent.'

'I'm really fond of it,' Skriva went on, as if speaking in parables.

'Who isn't?'

'Yar, who isn't? Gurd loves it, too. Most everybody does.' Skriva stopped, then added, 'In fact, the chump who doesn't love it is either daft or dead.'

'If you're leading up to something, say so,' Mowry urged. 'Cut out the song-and-dance act. We haven't got all day.'

'I know a fellow who loves money.'

'So what?'

'He's a jailer,' said Skriva pointedly.

Twisting sideways in his seat, Mowry eyed him carefully. 'Let's get down to brass tacks. What's he willing to do, and how much does he want?'

'He says Gurd's in a cell along with a couple of old pals of ours. So far, none of them have been put through the mill – though they'll be worked over sooner or later. Fellows in clink are usually given plenty of time to think over what's coming to them. It helps them break down quicker.'

'That's the usual technique,' Mowry agreed. 'Let them become nervous wrecks before making them physical wrecks.'

'Yar, the stinking *sokos*.' Skriva spat out of the window before he continued. 'Whenever a prisoner's number comes up, the Kaitempi call at the jail, present an official demand for him and take him to their HQ for treatment. Sometimes they bring him back several days later; by then, he's a cripple. Sometimes they don't bring him back. Then they file a death warrant to keep the prison records straight.'

'Go on.'

'This fellow who loves money will give me the number and location of Gurd's cell. Also the timing of Kaitempi visits and full details of their routine. And most important, he'll get a copy of the official form used for demanding release.' He let that sink in, finished, 'He wants a hundred thousand.'

Mowry pursed his lips in a silent whistle. 'You think we should try to get Gurd out?'

'Yar.'

'Didn't know you were so fond of him.'

'He could stay there and rot for all I care,' said Skriva. 'He's stupid. Why should I worry about him, *hi?*'

'All right, let him stay and rot. We'll save a hundred thousand that way.'

'Yar,' Skriva approved. 'But . . .'

'But what?'

'I could use the dope and the two with him. So could you, if you've got more work in mind. And if Gurd's kept in they'll make him talk – and he knows too much . . . And what's a hundred thousand to you?'

'Too much to throw away on a fancy story,' Mowry told him bluntly. 'Prize fool I'd be to hand you a huge wad just because you say Gurd's in the clink.'

Skriva's face darkened. 'You don't believe me, *hi?*'

'I've got to be shown,' said Mowry, undisturbed.

'Maybe you'd like a special tour through the jail and have Gurd pointed out to you?'

'The sarcasm is wasted. You seem to forget that while Gurd may be able to put the finger on you for fifty or more major crimes, he can do nothing whatsoever about me. He can talk himself black in the face without saying anything worth a hoot so far as I am concerned. No, when I spend money it'll be *my* money and it'll be spent for *my* reasons, not yours.'

'So you won't splurge a guilder on Gurd?'

'I didn't say that. I won't throw money away for nothing, but I'm willing to pay for full value received.'

'Meaning what?'

'Tell this money-loving screw that we'll give him twenty thousand for a genuine Kaitempi requisition form – *after* he has handed it over. Also that we'll pay him a further eighty thousand *after* Gurd and his two companions have got away.'

A mixture of expressions crossed Skriva's unlovely features – surprise, gratification, doubt, and puzzlement. 'What if he won't play on these terms?'

'He stays poor.'

'Well, what if he agrees but won't believe I can find the money? How do I convince him?'

'Don't bother to try,' Mowry advised. 'He has to speculate in order to accumulate, same as everyone else. If he won't do it, let him remain content with grinding poverty.'

'Maybe he'd rather stay poor than take the risk.'

'He won't. He's running no real risk and he knows it. There's only one chance he could take, and he'll avoid that.'

'Such as?'

'Suppose we arrive to make the rescue and are jumped on before we can open our mouths, or show the requisition form, what will it prove? It'll show that this fellow fooled you for the sake of the reward. The Kaitempi will pay him five thousand apiece for laying the trap and tipping them off. He'll make an easy and legal ten thousand on top of the twenty thousand we've already paid him. Correct?'

'Yar,' said Skriva uneasily.

'But he'll lose the eighty thousand yet to come. The difference is big enough to ensure his absolute loyalty up to the moment he gets it in his hot little hands.'

'Yar,' repeated Skriva, brightening considerably.

'After that – *zunk!*' said Mowry. 'As soon as he's got his claws on the lot, we'd better run like hell.'

'Hell?' Skriva stared at him. 'That's a Spakum curse-word.'

Mowry sweated a bit as he replied offhandedly, 'So it is. One picks up all sorts of bad language in wartime, especially on Diracta.'

'Ah, yes, on Diracta,' echoed Skriva, mollified. He got out of the car. 'I'll go see this jailer. We'll have to move fast. Phone me this time tomorrow, *hi?*'

'All right.'

The next day's work was the easiest to date, though not devoid of danger. All he had to do was gossip to anyone willing to listen. This was in accordance with the step-by-step technique taught him by the college.

'First of all you must establish the existence of an internal opposition. It doesn't matter whether the opposition is real or imaginary, so long as the enemy becomes convinced of its actuality.'

He had done that much.

'Second, you must create fear of that opposition and provoke the enemy into striking back at it as best he can.'

He'd done that, too.

'Third, you must answer the enemy's blows with enough defiance to force him into the open, to bring his reaction to public attention and to create the general impression that the opposition has confidence in its own power.'

That also had been achieved.

'The fourth move is ours and not yours. We'll take enough military action to demolish the enemy's claims of invincibility. After that, public morale should be shaky.'

One bomb on Shugruma had done the shaking.

'You then take the fifth step by sowing rumours. Listeners will be ripe to absorb and spread them – and the stories will lose nothing in the telling. A good rumour, well planted and thoroughly disseminated, can spread alarm and despondency over a wide area. But be careful in your choice of victims. If you pick on a fanatical patriot, it may be the end of you!'

In any city, in any part of the cosmos, the public park is a natural haunt of idlers and gossips. That is where James Mowry went in the morning. The benches were occupied almost entirely by elderly people. Young folk tended to keep clear of such places, lest inquisitive cops ask why they were not at work.

Selecting a seat next to a gloomy-looking oldster with a perpetual sniff, Mowry contemplated a bed of tattered flowers until the other turned toward him and said conversationally, 'Two more gardeners have gone.'

'So? Gone where?'

'Into the armed forces. If they draft the rest of them, I don't know what will happen to this park. It needs someone to look after it.'

'There's a lot of work involved,' agreed Mowry. 'But I suppose the war comes first.'

'Yar. Always the war comes first.' Sniffy said it with cautious disapproval. 'It should have been over by now. But it drags on and on. Sometimes I wonder when it will end.'

'That's the big question,' responded Mowry, making himself a fellow spirit.

'Things can't be going as well as they're said to be,' continued Sniffy morbidly, 'else the war would be over. It wouldn't drag on the way it does.'

'Personally, I think things are pretty bad.' Mowry hesitated, then went on confidingly, 'In fact, I know they are.'

'You do? Why?'

'Maybe I shouldn't tell you – but it's bound to come out sooner or later.'

'What is?' insisted Sniffy, consumed with curiosity.

'The terrible state of affairs at Shugruma. My brother came this morning and told me.'

'Go on – what did he say?'

'He tried to go there for business reasons but couldn't get to the place. A ring of troops turned him back forty *den* from the town. Nobody except the military, or salvage and medical services, is being allowed to enter the area.'

'That so?' said Sniffy.

'My brother says he met a fellow who'd escaped with nothing but the clothes he was wearing. This fellow told him that Shugruma was practically wiped off the map. Not one stone left upon another. Three hundred thousand dead. He said the scene is so awful that the newspapers daren't describe it – in fact, they refuse to mention it.'

Staring straight ahead, Sniffy said nothing but looked appalled.

Mowry added a few more lurid touches, brooded with him for a short time, and took his departure. All that he'd said would be repeated, he could be sure of that. A little later, and half a mile away, he had another on the hook – a beady-eyed, mean-faced character only too willing to hear the worst.

'Even the papers dare not talk about it,' Mowry ended.

Beady-eyes swallowed hard. 'If a single Spakum ship can dive in and drop a big one, so can a dozen others.'

'Yar, that's right.'

'In fact, they could have dropped more than one while they were at it. Why didn't they?'

'Maybe they were making a test run. Now that they know how easy it is, they'll come along with a *real* load. If that happens, there won't be much left of Pertane.' He pulled his right ear and made a *tzzk!* sound between his teeth, that being the Sirian equivalent of showing thumbs down.

'Somebody ought to do something about it,' declared Beady, unnerved.

'I'm going to do something myself,' informed Mowry. 'I'm going to dig myself a deep hole way out in the fields.'

He left the other half-paralysed with fright, took a short walk, then picked on a cadaverous individual who looked like a mortician on vacation.

'Close friend of mine – he's a fleet leader in the space-navy – told me confidentially that a Spakum onslaught has made Gooma completely uninhabitable. He thinks the only reason they haven't given Jaimec the same treatment is because they're planning to grab the place and naturally don't want to rob themselves of the fruits of victory.'

'Do you believe all that?' demanded the Embalmer.

'One doesn't know what to believe when the government tells you one thing and grim experience tells you another. It's only his personal opinion, anyway. But he's in the space-navy and knows a few things that we don't.'

'It has been stated authoritatively that the Spakum fleets have been destroyed.'

'Yar, they were still saying so when that bomb fell on Shugruma,' Mowry reminded him.

'True, true – I felt it land. In my own house two windows collapsed, and a bottle of *zith* jumped off the table.'

By mid-afternoon thirty people had been fed the tale of the Shugruma and Gooma disasters, plus allegedly first-hand warnings of bacteriological warfare and worse horrors to come. They could no more keep it to themselves than a man can keep

126

a tornado to himself. By early evening a thousand would have the depressing news.

At the arranged time he called Skriva. 'What luck?'

'I've got the form. Have you got the money?'

'Yar.'

'It's to be paid before tomorrow. Shall we meet same place as last?'

'No,' said Mowry. 'It is not wise to create a habit. Let's make it some other place.'

'Where?'

'There's a certain bridge where you collected once before. How about the fifth marker past it going south?'

'That's as good as anywhere. Can you go there at once?'

'I've got to pick up my car. It'll take a little time. You be there at the seven-time hour.'

James Mowry reached the marker on time, and found Skriva waiting. Handing over the money, he took the requisition form and examined it carefully. One good look told him that the thing was well-nigh impossible for him to copy. It was an ornate document, as lavishly engraved as a banknote of high denomination. They could cope with it on Terra, but the form was beyond his ability to duplicate – even with the help of various instruments of forgery lying in the cave.

The form was a used one, dated three weeks ago, and obviously had been purloined from the jail's filing system. It called for the release to the Kaitempi of one prisoner named Mabin Garud, but had enough blank spaces for ten names. The date, the prisoner's name and number had been typed. The authorizing signature was in ink.

'Now we've got it,' prompted Skriva, 'what are we going to do with it?'

'We can't imitate it,' Mowry informed. 'The job is too tough and will take too long.'

'You mean it's no use to us?' Skriva registered angry disappointment.

'I wouldn't say that.'

'Well, what do you say? Am I to give this stinker his twenty thousand, or do I cram the form down his gullet?'

'You can pay him.' Mowry studied the form again. 'I think that if I work on it tonight I can erase the date, name, and number. The signature can be left intact.'

'That's risky. It's easy to spot erasures.'

'Not the way I do them. I know how to gloss the surface afterward. The really difficult task will be that of restoring the broken lines of engraving.' He pondered for a moment, went on, 'But that may not be necessary. There's a good chance the new typing will fill in the blanks. It's hardly likely that they'll put the form under a microscope.'

'If they were that suspicious, they'd grab us first,' Skriva pointed out.

'I need a typewriter. I'll have to buy one in the morning.'

'I can get you a typewriter for tonight,' offered Skriva.

'You can? How soon?'

'By the eight-time hour.'

'Is it in good condition?'

'Yar, it's practically new.'

Mowry eyed him. 'I suppose it's no business of mine, but I can't help wondering what use a typewriter is to *you*.'

'I can sell it. I sell all sorts of things.'

'Things you just happened to come across?'

'That's right,' grinned Skriva, unabashed.

'Oh well, who am I to quibble? You get it. Meet me here at eight.'

Skriva pushed off. When he'd gone from sight Mowry followed into the city. He ate, then drove back to the marker. Soon afterward Skriva reappeared and gave him the typewriter.

Mowry said, 'I want Gurd's full name and those of his two companions. Somehow or other you'll have to discover their prison numbers, too. Can you do that?'

'I've got them already.' Skriva took a slip of paper from his pocket and read them out while Mowry made notes.

'Did you also learn at what times the Kaitempi make their calls to collect?'

'Yar. Always between the three and four-time hours. Never earlier, rarely later.'

'Can you find out about noon tomorrow whether Gurd and the others are still in the jail? We've got to know that – we'll get ourselves in a fix if we arrive and demand prisoners who were taken away this afternoon.'

'I can check on it tomorrow.' Skriva's face tautened. 'Are you planning to get them away *tomorrow?*'

'We've got to do it sometime or not at all. The longer we leave it, the bigger the risk of the Kaitempi beating us to the draw. What's wrong with tomorrow, *hi?*'

'Nothing – I just wasn't counting on it being so soon.'

'Why?' asked Mowry.

'I thought it'd take longer to work things out.'

'There's little to work out. We've swiped a requisition form. We alter it and use it to demand release of three prisoners. Either we get away with it or we don't. If we do, well and good. If we don't, we shoot first and run fast.'

'You make it sound too easy,' Skriva objected. 'All we've got is this form. If it isn't enough . . .'

'It won't be enough, I can tell you that now. Chances are ten to one they'll expect familiar faces and be surprised by strange ones. We'll have to compensate for that somehow.'

'How?'

'Don't worry, we'll cope. Can you dig up a couple more helpers? All they need do is sit in the cars, keep their traps shut and look tough. I'll pay them five thousand apiece.'

'Five thousand each? I could recruit a regiment for that money. Yar, I can find two. But I don't know how good they'd be in a fight.'

'Doesn't matter, so long as they look like plug-uglies. By that I don't mean the Café Susun kind of roughneck, see? They've got to look like Kaitempi agents.' He gave the other an imperative nudge. 'The same applies to you. When it's time to start, I want to see all three of you clean and tidy, with well-pressed suits and neatly knotted neck-scarves. I want to see you looking as if you're about to attend a wedding. If you let me down on that, you can count me out and go pull the stunt on your own. I don't intend to try to kid any warden with the aid of three scruffy-looking bums.'

'Maybe you'd like us decked out in fashionable jewelry,' suggested Skriva sarcastically.

'A diamond on the hand is better than a smear of dirt,' Mowry retorted. 'It's better to overdo the dolling-up than to look like hobos. You'd get away with a splurge because some of these agents are flashy types.' He waited for comment, but the other said nothing. 'What's more, these two helpers had better be characters you can trust not to talk afterward – else they may take my five thousand and then get another five from the Kaitempi for betraying you.'

Skriva was on firm ground there. He gave an ugly grin and promised, 'One thing I can guarantee is that neither of them will say a word.'

This assurance bore a sinister undertone, but Mowry let it pass. 'Lastly, we'll need a couple of dynos. We can't use our own unless we change the plates. Any ideas on that?'

'Pinching a pair of dynos is as easy as taking a mug of *zith*. The trouble is keeping them for any length of time. The longer we use them, the bigger the chance of being picked up by some lousy patrol with nothing better to do.'

'We'll have to cut the use of them to the minimum,' Mowry told him. 'Take them as late as you can. We'll park our own cars on that lot the other side of the Asako Bridge. When we leave the jail we'll beat it straight there and switch.'

'Yar, that is best,' Skriva agreed.

'All right. I'll be waiting outside the east gate of the municipal park at the two-time hour tomorrow. You come along with two cars and two helpers and pick me up.'

At that point Skriva became strangely restless. He fidgeted around, opened his mouth, and shut it.

Watching him curiously, Mowry invited, 'Well, what's the matter? You want to call the whole thing off?'

Skriva mustered his thoughts and burst out with, 'Look, Gurd means nothing to you. The others mean even less. But you're paying good money and taking a big risk to get them out of clink. It doesn't make sense.'

'A lot of things don't make sense. This war doesn't make sense – but we're in it up to the neck.'

'Curses on the war. That has nothing to do with it.'

'It has everything to do with the matter,' Mowry contradicted. 'I don't like the war, and lots of others don't. If we kick the government often enough and hard enough, they won't like it, either.'

'Oh, so that's what you're up to?' Skriva stared at him in frank surprise. 'You're chivvying the authorities?'

'Any objections?'

'I couldn't care less,' informed Skriva, and added virtuously, 'Politics is a dirty game. Anyone who plays around in it is crazy. All it gets him in the end is a free burial.'

'It'll be my burial, not yours.'

'Yar, that's why I don't care.' Obviously relieved, Skriva finished, 'Meet you at the park tomorrow.'

'On time. If you're late, I won't be there.'

As before, James Mowry waited until the other had gone from sight before driving to town. It was a good thing, he thought, that Skriva had the criminal mentality. It simply wouldn't occur to him that there are criminals and there are traitors.

Any one of Skriva's bunch would turn his own mother over to the Kaitempi – not as a duty to the nation, but solely for five thousand guilders. Similarly, they'd hand Mowry over and pocket the cash with a hearty laugh. All that prevented them from selling him body and soul was the fact they'd freely admitted – one does not flood one's own gold mine.

Provided the cars and helpers could be obtained, Skriva would be there on time tomorrow. He felt sure of that.

ELEVEN

Exactly at the two-time hour, a big black dyno paused at the east gate, picked up Mowry, and whined onward. Another dyno, older and slightly battered, followed a short distance behind.

Sitting at the wheel of the first car, Skriva looked neater and more respectable than Mowry had imagined was possible. Skriva exuded a faint smell of scented lotion, and seemed self-conscious about it. With his gaze fixed firmly ahead, he jerked a manicured thumb over his shoulder to indicate a similarly washed and scented character in the back seat.

'Meet Lithar. He's the sharpest *wert* on Jaimec.'

Mowry twisted his head around and gave a polite nod. Lithar rewarded him with a blank stare. Returning his attention to the windshield, Mowry wondered what on earth a *wert* might be. He'd never heard the word before and dared not ask its meaning. It might be more than an item of local jargon – perhaps a slang word added to the Sirian language during the years he had been away. It wouldn't be wise to admit ignorance.

'The fellow in the other car is Brank,' said Skriva. 'He's a red-hot *wert*, too. Lithar's right-hand man. That so, Lithar?'

The sharpest *wert* on Jaimec responded with a grunt. To give him his due, he fitted the part of a Kaitempi agent of the surly type. In that respect, Skriva had chosen well.

Threading their way through a series of side streets, they reached a main road and found themselves held up by a long, noisy convoy of half-tracked vehicles crammed with troops. Perforce they stopped and waited. The convoy rolled on and on; Skriva began to curse under his breath.

'They're gaping around like newcomers,' observed Mowry. 'Must have just arrived from somewhere.'

'Yar, from Diracta,' Skriva told him. 'Six shiploads landed this morning. There's a story going the rounds that ten set out but only six got here.'

'That so? It doesn't look so good if they're rushing additional forces to Jaimec despite heavy losses *en route*.'

'Nothing looks good except a stack of guilders twice my height,' opined Skriva. He scowled at the rumbling half-tracks. 'If they delay us long enough, we'll still be here when a couple of boobs start bawling about their missing cars. The cops will find us just waiting to be grabbed.'

'So what?' said Mowry. 'Your conscience is clear, isn't it?'

Skriva answered that with a look of disgust. At last the procession of military vehicles came to an end. The car jolted forward as he rushed it impatiently into the road and built up speed.

'Take it easy,' Mowry advised. 'We don't want to be nailed for ignoring some petty regulation.'

At a point a short distance from the jail Skriva pulled in to the curb and parked. The other dyno stopped close behind. He turned toward Mowry. 'Before we go any farther, let's have a look at that form.'

Extracting it from a pocket, Mowry gave it to him. He pored over it, seemed satisfied, handed it to Lithar. 'Looks all right to me. What d'you think?'

Lithar eyed it impassively, gave it back. 'It's good enough or it isn't. You'll find out pretty soon.'

Sensing something sinister in this remark, Skriva said to Mowry, 'The idea is that a couple of us walk in, present this form and wait for them to fetch us the prisoners, *hi?*'

'Correct.'

'What if this form isn't enough, and they ask for proof of our identities?'

'I can prove mine.'

'Yar? What sort of proof?'

'Who cares, so long as it convinces them?' Mowry evaded. 'As for you, fix this inside your jacket and flash it if necessary.' He gave the other Sagramatholou's badge.

Fingering it in open surprise, Skriva demanded, 'Where'd you get this?'

'An agent gave it to me. I have influence, see?'

'You expect me to believe that? No Kaitempi *soko* would dream of . . .'

'It so happened that he had expired,' Mowry put in. 'Dead agents are very co-operative, as perhaps you've noticed.'

'You killed him?'

'Don't be nosy.'

'Yar, what's it to us?' interjected Lithar from the back seat. 'You're wasting time. Put a move on and let's get the whole thing over – or let's throw it up and get back home.'

Thus urged, Skriva started up and drove forward. Now that he was rapidly coming to the point of committing himself, his edginess was obvious. But it was too late to retreat. The jail was now in sight, its great steel doors set in high stone walls. Rolling towards the doors, the two cars stopped. Mowry got out. Skriva followed suit, thin-lipped and resigned.

Mowry thumbed the bell-button set in the wall. A small door which formed a section of the bigger one emitted metallic clankings and opened. Through it an armed guard eyed them questioningly.

'Kaitempi call for three prisoners,' announced James Mowry with becoming arrogance.

With a brief glance at the waiting cars and their *wert* occupants, the guard motioned the two inside, closed the door, slid home the bar. 'You're a little early today.'

'Yar, we've got a lot to do. We're in a hurry.'

'This way.'

They tramped after the guard in single file, Skriva last with a hand in a pocket. Taking them into the administration building, along a corridor and past a heavily barred sliding gate, the guard led them into a small room in which a burly, grim-faced Sirian was sitting behind a desk. Upon the desk stood a small plaque reading: *Commandant Tornik*.

'Three prisoners are required for immediate interrogation,' said Mowry officiously. 'Here is the requisition form, Commandant. We are pressed for time and would be obliged if you'd produce them as quickly as possible.'

Tornik frowned over the form but did not examine it closely. Dialing an intercom phone, he ordered somebody to bring the three to his office. Then he lay back in his chair and regarded the visitors with complete lack of expression.

'You are new to me.'

'Of course, Commandant. There is a reason.'

'Indeed? What reason?'

'It is believed that these prisoners may be more than ordinary criminals. We have reason to suspect them of being members of a revolutionary army, namely, *Dirac Angestun Gesept*. Therefore they are to be questioned by Military Intelligence as well as by the Kaitempi. I am the MI representative.'

'Is that so?' said Tornik. 'We have never had the MI here before. May I have evidence of your identity?'

Producing his documents, Mowry handed them over. This wasn't going so swiftly and smoothly as hoped for. Mentally he prayed for the prisoners to appear and put a quick end to the matter. It was obvious that Tornik was the type to fill in time so long as everyone was kept waiting.

After a brief scrutiny, Tornik returned the papers and commented, 'Colonel Halopti, this is somewhat irregular. The requisition form is quite in order, but I am supposed to hand prisoners over only to a Kaitempi escort. That is a very strict rule that cannot be disobeyed, even for some other branch of the security forces.'

'The escort *is* of the Kaitempi,' answered Mowry. He threw

an expectant look at Skriva, who was standing like one in a dream. Skriva came awake, opened his jacket and displayed the badge. Mowry added, 'They provided me with three agents, saying that their attendance was necessary.'

'Yar, that is correct.' Pulling open a drawer in his desk, Tornik produced a receipt form, filled it in by copying details from the requisition. When he had finished, he complained, 'I'm afraid I cannot accept your signature, Colonel. Only a Kaitempi official may sign a receipt for prisoners.'

'I'll sign it,' offered Skriva.

'But you have a badge and not a plastic card,' Tornik objected. 'You are only an agent, not an officer.'

Mowry interjected, 'He is of the Kaitempi and temporarily under my command. I am an officer, although not of the Kaitempi.'

'That is so, but . . .'

'A receipt for prisoners must be given by the Kaitempi and by an officer. Therefore the proper conditions will be fulfilled if both of us sign.'

Tornik considered this and decided that it agreed with the letter of the law. 'Yar, the regulations must be observed. You will both sign.'

Just then the door opened, and Gurd and his companions shuffled in with a rattle of wrist-chains. A guard followed, produced a key, unlocked the manacles and took them away. Gurd, now worn and haggard, kept his gaze on the floor and maintained a surly expression. One of the others, a competent actor, glowered at Tornik, Mowry, and Skriva in turn. The third beamed around in happy surprise until Skriva bared his teeth at him. The smile then vanished. Luckily neither Tornik nor the attendant guard noticed this byplay.

Mowry signed the receipt with a confident flourish; Skriva appended his hurried scrawl beneath. The three prisoners stood silently by, Gurd still moping, the second scowling, the third wearing the grossly exaggerated expression of one in mourning for a rich aunt. Number three, Mowry decided, was definitely a dope who'd ham his way to an early grave.

'Thank you, Commandant.' Mowry turned toward the door. 'Let's go.'

In shocked tones, Tornik exclaimed, 'What, without wrist-chains, Colonel? Have you brought no manacles with you?'

Gurd stiffened; number two bunched his fists; number three made ready to faint. Skriva stuck his hand back in his pocket and kept full attention on the guard.

Glancing back at the other, Mowry said, 'We have steel anklets fixed to the floors of the cars. That is the MI way, Commandant.' He smiled with the air of one who knows. 'A prisoner runs with his feet and not with his hands.'

'Yar, that is true,' Tornik conceded.

They went out, led by the guard who had brought them there. The prisoners followed, with Skriva and Mowry bringing up the rear. Through the corridor, past the barred gate, out the main door and across the yard. Armed guards patrolling the wall-top eyed them indifferently. Five pairs of ears strained for a yell of fury and a rush of feet from the administration building; five bodies were tensed in readiness to slug the guard and make a dash for the exit door.

Reaching the wall, the guard grasped the locking-bar in the small door – and just then the bell was rung from outside. This sudden, unexpected sound jolted their nerves. Skriva's gun came halfway out of his pocket. Gurd took a step toward the guard, his expression vicious. The actor jumped as if stung. Dopey opened his mouth to emit a yelp of fright, converted it into a gargle as Mowry rammed a heel on his foot.

Only the guard remained undisturbed. With his back to the others, unable to see their reactions, he lugged the locking-bar to one side, turned the handle, opened the door. Beyond stood four sour-faced characters in plain clothes.

One of them said curtly, 'Kaitempi call for one prisoner.'

For some reason best known to himself, the guard found nothing extraordinary about two collecting parties turning up in close succession. He motioned the four inside, held the door open while the first arrivals went out. The newcomers did not head straight across the yard toward the administration block. They took a few steps in that direction, stopped as if by common consent, and stared at Mowry and the others as they passed. It was the dishevelled look of the prisoners and the chronic alarm on the face of Dopey that attracted their attention.

Just as the door shut, Mowry, who was last out, heard an agent rasp at the guard, 'Who are those, *hi?*'

The reply wasn't audible, but the question was more than enough. 'Jump to it!' Mowry urged. 'Run!'

They sprinted to the cars, spurred on by expectation of immediate trouble. A third machine now stood behind their two – a big ugly dyno with nobody at the wheel. Lithar and Brank watched them anxiously, opened the doors in readiness.

Scrambling into the leading dyno, Skriva started its motor while Gurd went through the back door and practically flung himself into Lithar's lap. Behind, the other two piled into the rear of Brank's car.

Mowry gasped at Skriva, 'Wait a moment while I see if I can grab theirs – it'll delay the chase.'

So saying, he raced to the third car, frantically tugged at its handle. It refused to budge. Just then the jail's door opened and somebody roared, 'Halt! Halt or we . . .' Brank promptly stuck an arm out of his open window and flicked four quick shots toward the door-gap. He missed each time, but it was sufficient to make the shouter dive for cover. Mowry pelted back to the leading dyno and fell in beside Skriva.

'The cursed thing is locked. Let's get out of here.'

The car surged forward, tore down the road. Brank accelerated after them. Watching through the rear window, Mowry saw several figures bolt out of the jail and waste precious moments fumbling by their dyno before they got in.

'They're after us,' he told Skriva. 'And they'll be bawling their heads off over the radio.'

'Yar, but they haven't got us yet.'

Gurd said, 'Did nobody think to bring a spare gun?'

'Take mine,' responded Lithar, handing it over.

Cuddling it in an eager fist, Gurd grinned at him unpleasantly. 'Don't want to be caught with it on you, *hi?* Typical *wert*, aren't you?'

'Shut up!' snarled Lithar.

'Look who's telling me to shut up,' Gurd invited. He was talking thickly, as if something had gone wrong with his palate. 'He's making a stack of money out of me, else he wouldn't be here at all. He'd be safe at home checking his stocks of illegal *zith* while the Kaitempi belted me over the gullet. And he tells me to shut up.' Leaning forward, he tapped Mowry on the shoulder with the barrel of the gun. 'How much is he making out of this, Mashambigab? How much are you giving . . .'

He swayed wildly and clutched for a hold as the car rocked around a corner, raced down a narrower road, turned sharp right and then sharp left. Brank's car took the same corner at the same speed, made the right turn but not the left one; it rushed straight on and vanished from sight. They turned again into a one-way alley, cut through to the next road. There was now no sign of pursuit.

'We've lost Brank,' Mowry told Skriva. 'Looks like we've dropped the Kaitempi, too.'

'It's a safe bet they're chasing Brank. They were closer to him and they had to follow someone when we split up. Suits us, doesn't it?'

Mowry said nothing.

'A lousy *wert* tells *me* to shut up,' mumbled Gurd.

Swiftly they zigzagged through a dozen side streets, still without encountering a radio-alarmed patrol-car. As they squealed around the last corner – near the place where their own cars were parked – a sharp, hard crack sounded in the rear. Mowry looked back, expecting to find a loaded cruiser closing up on them. There was no car behind. Lithar was lying on his side apparently asleep. He had a neat hole above his right ear; a thin trickle of purplish blood was seeping out of it.

Gurd smirked at Mowry and said, 'I've shut *him* up, for keeps.'

'Now we're carrying a corpse,' complained Mowry. 'As if we haven't trouble enough. Where's the sense . . .'

Skriva interrupted with, 'Crack shots, the Kaitempi. Pity they got Lithar – he was just the sweetest *wert* on Jaimec.'

He braked hard, jumped out, ran across the lot and clambered into his own dyno. Gurd followed, the gun openly in his hand and not caring who noticed it.

Mowry stopped by the window as the machine started up. 'What about Brank?'

'What about him?' echoed Skriva.

'If we both beat it, he'll get here and find no chance to switch over.'

'What, in a city crammed with dynos?' He let the car edge forward. 'Brank's not here. That's his woe. Let him cope with his own troubles. We're beating it someplace safe while the going is good. You follow us.'

With that, he drove off. Mowry gave him a four hundred yard lead, then droned along behind while the distance between them slowly increased. Should he let Skriva lead him to a hide-out? There seemed little point in following to yet another rathole. The jail job had been done, and he'd achieved his purpose of stirring up a greater ruckus. There were no *werts* to pay off; Brank was lost, and Lithar was dead. If he wanted to regain contact with Gurd and Skriva, he could use that telephone number; or if, as was likely, it was no longer valid he could employ their secret post office under the marker.

Other considerations also urged him to drop the brothers for the time being. For one, the Colonel Halopti identity wouldn't be worth a hoot after the authorities wasted a few hours checking through official channels to establish its falsity. That would be by nightfall at latest. Once again, Pertane was becoming too hot to hold James Mowry; he'd better get out before it was too late.

For another thing, he was overdue to beam a report, and

Mowry's conscience was bothering him about his refusal to do so last time. If he didn't send one soon, he might never be able to transmit one at all. And Terra was entitled to be kept informed.

By this time the other car had shrunk with distance. Turning off to the right, he circled back into the city. At once he noticed a great change of atmosphere. There were far more police on the streets, and now their number had been augmented by fully armed troops. Patrol-cars swarmed like flies, though none saw fit to stop and question him. There were fewer pedestrians on the sidewalks than usual, and these hurried along looking furtive, fearful, grim or bewildered.

Stopping by the curb, outside a business block, Mowry lolled in his seat as if waiting for someone while he watched what was taking place on the street. The police, some uniformed and some in plain clothes, were all in pairs. The troops were in groups of six. Their sole occupation appeared to be that of staring at everyone who passed by, holding up any individual whose looks they didn't like, questioning and searching him. They also took particular note of cars, studying the occupants and eyeing the plate-numbers.

In the time that Mowry sat there, he and his car were given the sharp look-over at least twenty times. He endured it with an air of complete boredom and evidently passed muster, because no one questioned him. But that couldn't go on forever; some-one more officious than the rest would pick on him, merely because the others had not done so. He was tempting fate by staying there.

So he moved off, driving carefully to avoid the attention of numerous cruisers. Something had broken loose, no doubt of that; it was written on the gloomy faces all around. He wondered whether the government had been driven to admit a series of reverses in the space-war. Or perhaps the rumours he'd spread about Shugruma had come close enough to the truth to make authority concede the facts. Or maybe a couple of exceedingly important bureaucrats had tried to open mailed packages and splattered themselves over the ceiling, thus creating a tremendous wave of panic among the powers that be. One thing was certain: the recent jail break could not be solely responsible for the present state of affairs, though possibly it may have been the trigger.

Slowly he made his way into the run-down quarter where his room was located, determined to pick up his belongings and clear out as quickly as possible. The car nosed its way into his street. As usual, a group of idlers loafed on the corner and stared at Mowry as he went by. But something wasn't quite right about them. Their ill-kept clothes and careless postures gave them the superficial appearance of bums, but they were a little too well-fed, their gaze a bit too haughty.

The hair itched on the back of his neck, and he felt a peculiar thrill down his spine; but Mowry kept going, trying to look as if this street were only part of a tiresome drive and meant nothing to him whatsoever. Against a lamp-post leaned two brawny specimens without jackets or scarves; nearby, four more were shoring a wall. Six were gossiping around an ancient, decrepit truck, parked opposite the house where he had a top room. Three more were in the doorway of the house. Every one of these gave him the long, hard look as he rolled by with an air of total indifference.

The entire street was staked out, though it didn't look as if they had a detailed description of him. He could be wrong in this belief, deluded by an overactive imagination, but instinct told him that the street was covered from end to end. His only chance of escape lay in driving on, non-stop, and displaying complete lack of interest. He did not dare look at his house for evidence of a Radine-type explosion; just that small touch of curiosity might have been enough to bring the whole lot into action.

Altogether, he counted more than forty beefy strangers lolling around the road and doing their best to look shiftless. As he neared the street's end, four of them came out of a doorway and walked to the curb. Their attention was his way, their manner that of those about to stop him on general principles.

Promptly he braked and pulled in near two others who were squatting on a doorstep. He lowered the window and stuck his head out. One of the sitters got to his feet, came toward him.

'Pardon,' said Mowry apologetically. 'I was told first right and second left for Asako Road. It has got me here. I must have gone wrong somewhere.'

'Where were you told?'

'Outside the militia barracks.'

'Some people don't know one hand from the other,' opined this character. 'It should have been first left, second right – turn right again after going through the archway.'

'Thanks. One can lose a lot of time in a city this size.'

'Yar, especially when dopes point with the wrong hand.' The informant returned to his doorstep, sat down; he had not nursed even a dim suspicion.

Evidently they were not on the watch for someone easily recognizable – or, at any rate, not for someone who looked exactly like Colonel Halopti. It could be that they were in ambush for another badly wanted specimen who happened to live in this street. But he dared not put the matter to the test by returning to the house and going up to his room.

Ahead, the four who'd waited at the curb had now resumed their leaning against the wall, lulled by Mowry's open conversation with their fellows. They ignored him as he drove past. Turning right, he thankfully speeded up; but he had still a long way to go and the city had become one gigantic trap.

Near the city's outskirts, a patrol-car waved him down. For a moment, he debated whether to obey or try to outrace it; he decided in favour of the former. Bluff had worked before, and might do so again. Besides, to run for it would be a complete giveaway and every cruiser in the area would take up the chase.

The car drew alongside and the co-driver dropped his window. 'Where are you heading for?'

'Palmare,' answered Mowry, naming a village twenty *den* south of Pertane.

'That's what you think. Don't you listen to the news?'

'I haven't heard it since early this morning. Been too busy even to get a square meal. What's happened?'

'All exits barred. Nobody allowed out the city except with a permit from the military. You'd better go back and get yourself informed. Or buy an evening paper.'

The window went up and the patrol-car whined into top speed. James Mowry watched it go with mixed emotions. Again he was sharing all the sensations of a hunted animal.

He cruised around until he found a news-stand carrying the latest editions still damp from the press. He parked, got out and bought a copy, then sat in the car while he scanned the headlines.

PERTANE UNDER MARTIAL LAW

TRAVEL BAN – MAYOR DECLARES POPULATION WILL STAND FIRM

DRASTIC ACTION AGAINST DIRAC ANGESTUN GESEPT

POLICE ON TRAIL OF MAIL BOMBERS

TWO KILLED, TWO CAPTURED IN DARING JAILBREAK

Rapidly he read the brief report under the last heading. Lithar's body had been found, and the Kaitempi had grabbed the credit for the kill. That made Skriva something of a prophet; Dopey had been shot to death, while Brank and the other had been taken alive. The two survivors had confessed to membership in a revolutionary force. There was no mention of any others having got away, and nothing about the mock Colonel Halopti.

Probably authority had clamped down on some items in the

hope of giving the escapees a sense of false security. Well, from now on he must not show his documents to any cop or Kaitempi agent. Neither could he substitute any other papers. The only ones near to hand were locked in his case and surrounded by a horde of agents. The only others were in the forest cave, with a ring of troops between here and there.

A ring of troops? Yes, that could be a weak point that he might break through. It was probable that the numerically strong armed forces were not yet as well-primed as were the police and Kaitempi. The chance of being cross-examined and bullied came only from an individual of equal or higher rank. He could not imagine any colonels or major-generals manning the roadblocks. Anyone outranking a junior lieutenant was more likely to be warming an office chair, or boozing and boasting in the nearest *zith*-parlour.

Mowry decided that here lay his best opportunity to break out of the net.

About sixty routes radiated from the perimeter of Pertane. The main ones – such as the wide, well-used roads to Shugruma and Radine – were likely to be more heavily guarded than the secondary roads, or the potholed lanes leading to villages and isolated factories. It was also possible that the biggest, most important roadblocks would have a few police or agents in company with the troops.

Many of the lesser outlets were quite unknown to him; a random choice might take him into the fire. But not far away lay a little-used side road to Palmare. Mowry knew this road. It twisted and wound in a direction more or less parallel with the big main road, but it got there. Once on it, he could not get off it for another forty *den*. He'd have to continue all the way to Palmare, turn there onto a rutted cross-country lane that would take him to the Valapan road. At that point he'd be about half an hour's drive from the point where he usually entered the forest.

Cutting through the suburbs, he headed outward toward

this lesser road. Houses gradually thinned away and ceased. As he drove through a market-gardening area, a police cruiser whined toward him and passed without pause. He expelled a sigh of relief as it disappeared. Presumably it had been in too great a hurry to bother with him; or perhaps its occupants had assumed that he possessed a military permit.

Five minutes later, he rounded a blind corner and found a roadblock awaiting him two hundred yards beyond, A couple of army trucks stood side-on across the road, in such a position that a car could pass only if it slowed to less than walking pace. In front of the trucks a dozen soldiers stood in line, coddling their automatic weapons and looking bored. There was no cop or agent anywhere in sight.

Mowry slowed, stopped, but kept his dynomotor rotating. The soldiers eyed him with bovine curiosity. From behind the nearest truck a broad, squat sergeant appeared.

'Have you got an exit permit?'

'Don't need one,' responded Mowry, speaking with the authority of four-star general. Opening his wallet, he displayed his identity card and prayed that the sight of it would not produce a howl of triumph.

It didn't. The sergeant looked at it, stiffened, saluted; noticing this, the nearby troops straightened themselves and assumed expressions of military alertness.

In apologetic tones the sergeant said, 'I regret that I must ask you to wait a moment, Colonel. My orders are to report to the officer in charge if anyone claims the right to go through without a permit.'

'Even the Military Intelligence?'

'It has been emphasized that this order covers everyone without exception, sir. I have no choice but to obey.'

'Of course, Sergeant,' agreed Mowry condescendingly. 'I will wait.'

Saluting again, the sergeant went at the double behind the trucks. Meanwhile, the twelve troopers posed with the rigid self-consciousness of those aware of a brass hat in the vicinity.

In a short time the sergeant came back, bringing with him a very young and worried-looking lieutenant.

This officer marched precisely up to the car, saluted, and opened his mouth just as James Mowry beat him to the draw by saying. 'You may stand easy, Lieutenant.'

The other gulped, let his legs relax, fumbled for words, finally got out, 'The sergeant tells me you have no exit permit – Colonel.'

'That's right. Have you got one?'

Taken aback, the lieutenant floundered a bit, then said, 'No, sir.'

'Why not?'

'We are on duty outside the city.'

'So am I,' informed Mowry.

'Yes, sir.' The lieutenant pulled himself together. He seemed unhappy about something. 'Will you be good enough to let me see your identity card, sir? It is just a formality. I'm sure that everything will be all right.'

'I know that everything will be all right,' said Mowry, as though giving fatherly warning to the young and inexperienced. Again he displayed the card.

The lieutenant gave it no more than a hurried glance, 'Thank you, Colonel. Orders are orders, as you will appreciate.' Then he curried favour by demonstrating his efficiency. He took one step backward and gave a classy salute, which Mowry acknowledged with a vague wave. Jerking himself around like an automaton, the lieutenant brought his right foot down with a hard thump and screamed at the top of his voice, 'Pass one!'

Opening out, the troops obediently passed one. Mowry crawled through the block, curving around the tail of the first truck, twisting the opposite way around the second. Once, through, he hit up maximum speed. It was a temptation to feel gleeful, but he didn't, he was sorry for that young lieutenant. It was easy to picture the scene when a senior officer arrived at the post to check up.

'Anything to report, Lieutenant?'

'Not much, sir. No trouble of any sort. It has been very quiet. I let one through without a permit.'

'You did? Why was that?'

'He was Colonel Halopti, sir.'

'Halopti? That name seems familiar I'm sure I heard it mentioned as I left the other post.'

'He is in the MI, sir.'

'Yar, yar. But that name means something. Why don't they keep us properly informed? Have you a short-wave set?'

'Not here, sir. There is one at the next main road block. We have a field telephone.'

'All right, I'll use that.' A little later, 'You imbecile! This Halopti is wanted all over the planet! And you let him slip through your hands – you ought to be shot! How long has he been gone? Did he have anyone with him? Will he have passed through Palmare yet? Sharpen your wits, fool, and answer me! Did you note the number of his car? No, you did not – that would be too much to expect.'

And so on and so on. Yes, the balloon would go up almost any time; perhaps in three or four hours, perhaps within ten minutes. The thought of it made Mowry maintain what was a reckless speed on such a twisting and badly surfaced road.

He shot through small and sleepy Palmare, half-expecting to be fired upon by local vigilantes. Nothing happened except that a few faces glanced out of windows as he went by. Nobody saw him turn off the road a little beyond the village and take to the crude track that led to the Pertane-Valapan artery.

Now he was compelled to slow down, whether he liked it or not. Over that terrible surface the car bumped and rolled at quarter speed. If anything came the other way, he'd be in a jam, because there was no room to pull aside or turn. Two jet planes moaned through the gathering dusk, but carried straight on, indifferent to what was taking place below. Soon afterward a 'copter came low over the horizon, followed it a short distance, dropped back and disappeared. Its course showed that it was circling around Pertane, possibly checking the completeness of military positions.

Eventually Mowry reached the Pertane-Valapan route, without having encountered anything on the track. Accelerating, he made for the forest entry-point. A number of army vehicles trundled heavily along, but there was no civilian traffic to or from distant Pertane. Those inside the city could not get out; those outside did not want to go in.

At the moment he reached the identifying tree and tombstone, the road was clear in both directions. Taking full advantage of the opportunity, he drove straight over the verge and into the forest as far as the car could go. Jumping out, he went back and repeated his former performance eliminating all tyre tracks where they entered the forest and making sure that the car was invisible from the road.

The dark of night now was halfway across the sky. That meant he had to face another badly slowed-down hike to the cave. Alternatively he could sleep overnight in the car and start his journey with the dawn. The latter was preferable; even a wasp needs rest and slumber. On the other hand, the cave was more peaceful, more comfortable, and a good deal safer than the car. There he could enjoy a real Terran breakfast, after which he could lie full length and sleep like a child. He started for the cave at once, trying to make the most use of the fading light while it lasted.

With the first streaks of morning, James Mowry came wearily and red-eyed through the last of the trees. His finger-ring had been tingling for fifteen minutes, so that he made his approach with confidence. Clumping along the pebble beach, he went into the cave, and fixed himself a hearty meal. Then he crawled into a sleeping bag. The transmission of his report could wait. It would have to wait: communication might bring instructions impossible to carry out before he'd had a good spell of shut-eye.

He must have needed it, because dusk again was creeping in when he awoke. Setting up another meal, he ate it, felt on top of the world, expressed it by flexing his muscles and whistling badly off key.

For a while, Mowry studied the massed containers and nursed a few regrets. In one of them reposed material for repeated changes of appearance, plus documents, to cover no less than thirty more fake identities. The situation being what it was, he'd be lucky to get through three of them. Another container held publicity material, including the means to print and mail more letters.

> *Ait Lithar was the fifth.*
> *The list is long.*
> *Dirac Angestun Gesept.*

But what was the use? The Kaitempi had claimed that kill; moreover he needed to know the names of any mail bomb victims, so that *DAG* could exploit those, too. He lacked this information. Anyway, the time for that kind of propaganda was past. The entire world was on the jump; reinforcements had been poured in from Diracta; battle-stations had been taken up against a revolutionary army that did not exist. In such circumstances, threatening letters had become mere fleabites.

Dragging out Container-5, he set it up, wound it into action and let it run. For two and a half hours it operated silently.

Whirrup-dzzt-pam! Whirrup-dzzt-pam!

'Jaimec calling! Jaimec calling!'

Contact was established when the gravelly voice said, 'Come in. Ready to tape.'

Mowry responded, 'JM on Jaimec,' then babbled on as fast as he could go and to considerable length. He finished, 'Pertane isn't tenable until things quiet down, and I don't know how long that will take. Personally, I think the panic will spread to other towns. When they can't find what they're seeking in one place, they'll start raking systematically through all the others.'

There was a long silence before the faraway voice came back

with, 'We don't want things to quiet down. We want them to spread. Get working at once on phase nine.'

'Nine?' he ejaculated. 'I'm only on four. What about five, six, seven and eight?'

'Forget them. Time is running short. There's a ship getting near to you with another wasp on board. We sent him to tend to phase nine, thinking you'd been nabbed. Anyway, we'll beam instructions that he's to stay on the ship while we pick him another planet. Meanwhile, you get busy.'

'But phase nine is strictly a pre-invasion tactic.'

'That's right,' said the voice drily. 'I just told you time is running short.'

It cut off. Communication had ended. Mowry stacked the cylinder back in the cave; then he went outside and gazed at the stars.

TWELVE

Phase nine was designed to bring about a further dispersal of the enemy's overstretched resources, and to place yet another great strain upon his creaking war-machine. It was, so to speak, one of several possible last straws.

The idea was to make panic truly planet-wide by spreading it from land to water. Jaimec was peculiarly susceptible to this kind of blow. On a colonial world populated by only one race, of only one species, there had been no national or international rivalries, no local wars; no development of navies. The nearest that Jaimec could produce to a seagoing force consisted of a number of fast motorboats, lightly armed and used solely for coastal patrol work.

Even the merchant fleet was small by Terran standards. Jaimec was underdeveloped: no more than six hundred ships sailed the planet's seas on about twenty well-defined routes.

There wasn't a vessel larger than fifteen thousand tons. Nevertheless, the local war effort was critically dependent upon the unhampered coming and going of these ships. To delay their journeys, or ruin their schedules, or bottle them up in port, would raise considerable hob with the entire Jaimecan economy.

This sudden switch from phase four to phase nine meant that the oncoming Terran spaceship must be carrying a load of periboobs, which it would scatter in the world's oceans before making a quick getaway. Almost certainly the dropping would be done by night, and along the known sea-lanes.

At college, James Mowry had been given full instruction about this tactic and the part he was expected to play. The stunt had much in common with his previous activities, being designed to make a thoroughly irritated foe strike out in all directions at what wasn't there.

He'd been shown a sectionalized periboob. This deceitful contraption resembled an ordinary oildrum, with a twenty-foot tube projecting from its top. At the uppermost end of the tube was fixed a flared nozzle. The drum portion held a simple magneto-sensitive mechanism. The whole thing could be mass-produced at low cost.

When in the sea, a periboob floated so that its nozzle and four to six feet of tube stood above the surface. If a mass of steel or iron approached to within four hundred yards of it, the mechanism operated and the whole gadget sank from sight. If the metal mass receded, the periboob promptly rose until again its tube poked above the waves.

To function efficiently, this gadget needed a prepared stage and a spotlight. The former had been arranged by permitting the enemy to get hold of top-secret plans of a three-man midget submarine, small enough and light enough for an entire flotilla to be transported in one spaceship. Mowry now had to provide the spotlight by making a couple of merchant vessels sink at sea, after a convincing bang.

Jaimecans were as capable as anyone else of adding two and nothing together and making it four. If everything went as planned, the mere sight of a periboob would make any ship race for safety, filling the ether with yells for help. Other ships, hearing the alarm, would make wide, time-wasting detours, or would tie up in port. The dockyards would switch frantically from the building and repair of cargo vessels to the construction of useless destroyers. Numberless jet planes, 'copters, and even space-scouts would take over the futile task of patrolling the oceans and bombing periboobs.

The chief beauty of this was that it made no difference if the enemy discovered he was being suckered. He could trawl a periboob from the depths, take it apart, demonstrate how it worked to every ship's master on the planet – and it wouldn't matter. If two ships had been sunk, two hundred more might go down. A periscope is a periscope; there's no swift way of telling the false from the real, and no captain in his right mind will invite a torpedo while trying to find out.

Alapertane (little Pertane) was the biggest and nearest port on Jaimec. It lay forty *den* west of the capital, seventy *den* northwest of the cave: population a quarter of a million. It was very likely that Alapertane had escaped most of the official hysteria, that its police and Kaitempi were less suspicious, less active. Mowry had never visited the place and therefore neither had *Dirac Angestun Gesept*. So far as Alapertane was concerned, he had little grief to inherit.

Well, Terra knew what it was doing and orders must be carried out. He would have to make a trip to Alapertane and get the job done as soon as possible. He would go on his own, without Gurd and Skriva, who – so long as the hunt was on – remained dangerous liabilities.

Opening a container, Mowry took out a thick wad of documents, thumbed through them, and considered the thirty identities available. All of them had been devised to suit specific tasks. There were half a dozen that established his right to roam around the docks and peer at shipping. He chose a set of papers that depicted him as a minor official of the Planetary Board of Maritime Affairs.

Next, he made himself up for the part; it took him more than an hour. When finished, he was an elderly, bookish bureaucrat peering through steel-rimmed spectacles. That done, he amused himself by blinking at his image in a metal mirror and talking nonsense in characteristically querulous tones.

Long hair would have perfected his appearance, since he still had the short military crop of Halopti. A wig was out of the question; except for spectacles, the strict rule of facial disguise was to wear nothing that could be knocked, blown, or taken off.

So he shaved a patch of cranium to suggest approaching baldness and left it at that.

Finally he found himself another case, inserted its plastic key and opened it. Despite all the risks he had taken, and might take again, this was the act he dreaded most. He could never get rid of the notion that explosive luggage was highly temperamental, and that many a wasp had been blown to the nether regions with a phantom key in his hand.

From yet another container he took three limpet mines – two for use, and one as a spare. These were hemispherical objects with a heavy magnetic ring projecting from the flat side, and a timing-switch on the opposite, curved side. They weighed eleven pounds apiece, making a load he'd rather have been without. Putting these in the case, he stuffed a pocket with new money and checked his gun. Switching Container-22, he set forth.

By now, James Mowry was becoming more than fed up with the long, trying journey from the cave to the road. It hadn't looked much on an aerial photograph, when seen through a stereoscopic viewer, but the actual travelling was tough – especially in the dark when he was carrying a load.

He reached the car in broad daylight, thankfully dumped the case on the back seat, and checked the road for passing vehicles. The coast was clear. Racing back to the car, he got it out fast, parked it while he scuffed tyre tracks from the verge, then headed for Alapertane.

Fifteen minutes later, he was compelled to pull up. The road was filled with a convoy of army vehicles that were bucking and rocking as they reversed one by one into a treeless space. Troops who had dismounted were filtering in ragged lines between the trees on both sides of the road. A dozen glum civilians were sitting in one truck with four soldiers to guard them.

As Mowry sat watching, a captain came alongside the car and asked, 'Where're you from?'

'Valapan.'

'Where d'you live?'

'Kiestra, just outside Valapan.'

'Where're you going?'

'Alapertane.'

This seemed to satisfy the other. He started to move off.

Mowry called, 'What's happening here, Captain?'

'A round-up. We're collecting the windy and taking them back where they belong.'

'The windy?' Mowry looked baffled.

'Yar. The night before last, a lot of yellow-bellied *sokos* bolted out of Pertane and took to the woods. They were worried about their skins, see? More followed early yesterday morning. By now, half the city would be gone if we hadn't pinned them in. Civilians make me sick.'

'What got them on the run?'

'Talk.' He sniffed in contempt. 'Just a lot of talk.'

'Well, there's no rush from Valapan,' offered Mowry.

'Not yet,' the captain gave back. He walked away, bawled out a slow-moving squad.

The last trucks got off the road and Mowry forged ahead. Evidently the jailbreak had coincided with strong governmental action against a jittery populace. The city would have been ringed in any event.

Speculations about the fate of Gurd and Skriva occupied Mowry's mind as he drove along. As he passed through a village, he was tempted momentarily to stop, call their telephone number and see what response he got. He resisted the notion, but did pause long enough to buy a morning paper.

The news was little different – the usual mixture of boastings, threats, promises, directives, and warnings. One paragraph stated categorically that more than eighty members of *Dirac Angestun Gesept* had been hauled in, 'including one of their so-called generals.' He wondered which unfortunate character had been burdened with the status of revolutionary general. There was nothing about Gurd and Skriva, and no mention of Colonel Halopti.

Throwing the paper away, he continued his journey. Shortly before noon he reached the centre of Alapertane and asked a pedestrian the way to the docks. Though hungry once more, he did not take time off for a meal. Alapertane was not surrounded; no snap searches were taking place; no patrol-car had halted and quizzed him. He felt it wise to cash in on a favourable situation that might soon change for the worse, so he made straight for the waterfront.

Planting the dyno in the private car-park of a shipping company, he approached the gates of the first dock on foot, blinked through his spectacles at the policeman standing by the entrance and asked, 'Which way to the harbour master's office?'

The cop pointed. 'Right opposite the third set of gates.'

Going there James Mowry entered the office and tapped on the counter with the impatience of an oldster in a hurry.

A junior pen-pusher responded. 'You wish?'

Showing him his papers, Mowry said, 'I wish to know which ships will depart before dawn tomorrow, and from which docks they will leave.'

Obediently the other dug out a long, narrow book and sought through its pages. It did not occur to him to question the reason for this request. A piece of paper headed *Planetary Board of Maritime Affairs* was more than enough to satisfy him; as any fool knew, neither Alapertane nor its ships were menaced by the Spakum forces.

'Destinations as well?' asked the youth.

'No, those don't matter. I wish only the names, the times of departure, and the dock numbers.' Mowry produced a pencil and paper, and peered fussily over his glasses.

'There are four,' informed the other. 'The *Kitsi* at eight-time, dock three. The *Anthus* at eight-time, dock one. The *Su-cattra* at nineteen-time, dock seven. The *Su-limane* at nineteen-time, also dock seven.' He flipped a page and added, 'The *Melami* was due to leave at nineteen-time but is held up with some kind of trouble in the engine room. It is likely to be delayed several days.'

'That one doesn't matter.'

Leaving, Mowry returned to the car, got out the case, and went to dock seven. The policeman on duty took one look at his documents and let him through the gates without argument. Once inside, he walked quickly toward the long shed behind which towered a line of cranes and a couple of funnels. Rounding the end of the shed, he found himself facing the stern of the *Su-cattra*.

One glance told him that, at the present time, he had not the slightest hope of fixing a limpet-mine unseen. The vessel lay against the dockside, its hatches battened down, its winches silent; but many workers were hand-loading late cargo, carting it up the gangways from waiting trucks. A small mob of officials stood around watching. Across the basin lay the *Su-limane*, also taking cargo aboard.

For a short time, Mowry debated with himself whether to go after the *Anthus* and *Kisti*. There was the disadvantage that they were in different docks a fair distance apart; here, he had two suitable ships within easy reach of each other. And it was probable that the other vessels also were loading.

It seemed that, in his haste, he had arrived too early. The best thing for him to do would be to go away and come back later after workers and officials had gone home. But if the cop on the gate or a waterfront patrol became nosy, it would be hard to explain his need to enter the deserted dock area after all work had ceased. A hundred excuses could turn into a hundred self-betrayals.

'I have a personal message for the captain of the *Su-cattra*.'

'Yar? What is his name?'

Or, 'I have a corrected cargo manifest to deliver to the *Su-limane*.'

'Yar? Let me see it. What's the matter – can't you find it? How can you deliver it if you haven't got it? If it's not in your pockets, it may be in that bag. Why don't you look in the bag? You afraid to open it, *hi?*'

Leaving the dockside, Mowry walked past the end of the huge shed which stretched the entire length of the dock. Its sliding doors stood three feet ajar. He went through without hesitation. The side farthest from the dock was stacked roof-high with packing cases of every conceivable shape and size. The opposite side was part full. Near the main quayside doors, halfway up the shed, stood an array of cardboard cartons and bulging sacks which workers were taking out to the *Su-cattra.*

Seeing the name *Melami* stencilled all over the nearest stack of cargo, Mowry looked swiftly toward the distant loaders, assured himself that he had not been observed, and dodged behind a big crate. Though no longer visible from inside the shed, he could easily be seen by anyone passing the sliding doors through which he had entered. Holding his case endwise ahead of him, he inched through the narrow gap between two more crates, climbed over a big coffin-shaped box, and squirmed into a dark alcove between the stack and the shed's outer wall.

It was far from comfortable here. He could not sit; neither could he stand erect. He had to remain half-bent until, tired of that, he knelt on his case. But at least he was safe. The *Melami* was held up and nobody was likely to heave its cargo around for the fun of it.

He stayed there for what seemed a full day. The time came when whistles blew and sounds of outside activity ceased. Through the shed's wall sounded a muffled tramp of many feet as workers left for home. Nobody had bothered to close the shed's doors, and James Mowry couldn't make up his mind whether that was a good thing or not. Locked doors would suggest an abandoned dockside, guarded by none save the cop on the gate. Open doors implied the arrival of a night shift.

Edging out of the alcove, he sat on a crate and rubbed his aching kneecaps. He waited two more hours to let overtime workers and other eager beavers get clear. When his patience ran out, he walked through the deserted shed and stopped behind its quayside doors. These were directly opposite the middle of the *Su-cattra*.

From the case he took a limpet-mine, set its timing switch to give a twenty-hour delay, and threaded a length of thin cord through the holding loop. He peeped out of the door. There was not a soul on the dockside, but a few sailors were busy on the ship's top deck.

Boldly he stepped out of the shed, crossed the intervening ten yards and dropped the mine into the narrow stretch of water between ship and dockside. It hit with a dull plop and a slight splash, then sank rapidly to the limit of its cord. It was now about eight feet below the surface and did not immediately take hold. He waggled the cord to turn the magnetic face toward the ship. The mine promptly attached itself with a clang loud enough to resound all over the big vessel. Quickly he released one end of the cord, pulled on the other and reeled it in through the holding-loop.

High above him a sailor came to the rail, leaned on it and looked down. By that time, Mowry had his back to the man and was strolling casually toward the shed. The sailor watched him go inside, glanced at the stars, spat in the water, and went back to his chore.

Soon afterward, Mowry repeated the performance with the *Su-limane,* sticking the mine amidships and eight feet down. That one also had a twenty-hour delay. Again the clang aroused careless attention, bringing three curious sailors to the side. But they saw nobody and shrugged it off.

Mowry now made for the exit gates. On the way, he passed two officers returning to their ship. Engrossed in conversation, they did not so much as glance at him.

A different policeman was on duty by the gates as Mowry went through.

'Live long!'

'Live long!' echoed the cop, and turned his attention elsewhere.

Trudging a long way down the road, and rounding the corner near the gates of dock three, Mowry saw the car-park – and came to a halt. A hundred yards away, his car was standing exactly where he had left it; but its hood was raised and a couple of uniformed police were prying around the exposed dynomotor.

They must have unlocked the car with a master key in order to operate the hood's release catch. The fact they had gone to that length meant they were not amusing themselves by being officious. They were on a definite trail.

Retreating behind the corner, Mowry gave swift thought to the matter. Obviously those cops were looking for the dynomotor's serial number. In another minute, one of them would be crawling under the car to check the chassis number. This suggested that, at last, authority had realized that Sagramatholou's car had changed its plates; so the order had gone out to inspect all cars of that particular date and type.

Right in front of him, hidden from the car-park, stood an unoccupied cruiser. They must have left it there intending to edge it forward a few feet and use it as a watching-post if necessary. Once they'd satisfied themselves that the suspected dyno was indeed a hot one, they'd come back on the run to set a stakeout.

Cautiously, Mowry took a peep around the corner. One cop was talking excitedly, while the other scribbled in a notebook. It would be another minute before they returned, because they would close the hood and relock the dyno in order to bait the trap.

Certain that no passer-by would question something done with casual confidence. Mowry tried the cruiser's door-handle. It was locked. He had no key with which to open it, no time to pick it, and that put an end to any thought of taking one car in lieu of the other.

Opening his case, he took out the spare limpet-mine, and set it for a one-hour delay. He lay in the road, rapidly inched himself under the cruiser, and stuck the bomb to the centre of its steel framework. Wriggling out, he brushed himself down with his hands. Seven people had seen him go under and emerge; not one viewed his actions as extraordinary.

James Mowry snatched up his case and departed at a pace that was little short of a shambling run. At the next corner, he looked back. One cop was now sitting in the cruiser and using its shortwave radio. The other was out of sight, presumably concealed where he could watch the dyno. Evidently they were transmitting the news that the missing car had been found and were summoning help to surround it.

Again adverse circumstances were chivvying him into a tight corner. He had lost the car on which he had relied so much, and which had stood him in such good stead. All that he now possessed were his gun, a set of false documents, a large wad of counterfeit money, and a case that was empty save for what was wired to its lock.

The case he got rid of by placing it in the entrance to the main post office. That action would not help to cool things down. Discovery of his dyno had warned Alapertane that Sagramatholou's killer was somewhere within its bounds. While they were squatting around it in readiness to snare him, a police cruiser would shower itself all over the scene. Then somebody would dutifully take a lost case to the nearest precinct station; a cop would try to key it open, and make an awful mess of the place.

Alapertane already was half-awake. Two big bangs were going to bring it fully awake and on its toes; somehow he'd have to get out before they copied the Pertane tactic and ringed the town with troops.

THIRTEEN

This was a time when he regretted the destruction of Major Sallana's card in that explosion at Radine. Mowry could do with it now. Equally he was sorry that he'd given Sagramatholou's badge to Skriva. Despite the fact that James Mowry now looked as much like a Kaitempi agent as a purple porcupine, either the card or badge would have enabled him to commandeer any civilian car in town. He'd only have to order its driver to take him wherever he wished to go – shut up, and do as you're told.

There was one advantage: the hunters had no real description of Sagramatholou's killer. Perhaps they were shooting in the dark by seeking the elusive Colonel Halopti; or perhaps they were chasing a purely imaginary description which the Kaitempi had tormented out of its captives. It wasn't likely that they'd be sniffing around for an elderly, slightly befuddled civilian who wore glasses, and who was too daft to know one end of a gun from the other.

All the same, they would quiz anyone they caught leaving town in a hurry at this particular time, even if he looked the soul of innocence. They might go further by searching every outward traveller – in which event, Mowry would be damned by possession of a gun and a large sum of money. They might also hold any and every suspect, pending a thorough check of identities. That also would get the noose round Mowry's neck; the Board of Maritime Affairs had never heard of him.

Therefore, escape by train was out of the question. The

same applied to long-distance buses; they'd all be watched. Ten to one, the entire police network was ready to take up the relentless pursuit of any car reported stolen, they would assume that the culprit might have ditched one dyno, intending to steal another. It was too late in the day to acquire another car by buying it outright. But . . . hah, he could do what he'd done before; he could rent one.

It took him quite a while to find a hire-and-drive agency. The evening was drawing on; many businesses already had shut for the night, and others were near their closing time. In one way, that might be a help: maybe the lateness of the hour would cover his haste and get him prompt service.

'I wish to rent that bullnozed sportster for four days. Is it available at once?'

'Yar.'

'How much?'

'Thirty guilders a day. That's one-twenty.'

'I'll take it.'

'You want it right away?'

'Yar, I do.'

'I'll have it made ready for you and get you the bill. Take a seat. Won't keep you more than a few minutes.' The salesman went into a small office at the back. The door swung slowly and had not quite closed when his voice penetrated the gap, saying, 'A renter in a hurry, Siskra. He looks all right to me, but you'd better call and tell them.'

Mowry was out the front, down the street, and around two corners before the unseen Siskra had time to finish dialling. He'd been out-thought; the hunt was a move ahead of him. All renting agencies had been warned to report every applicant for a car. Only a narrow door-gap had saved him.

His back was sticky with sweat as he put distance between him and the dyno-dump. He threw away his glasses, and was glad to be rid of them. A bus came along bearing the sign: *Airport*. Now he remembered that he'd passed an airport on the road coming in; wasn't likely that Alapertane had more than one of them. Undoubtedly the port itself would be staked out, right, left, and centre, but he did not intend to ride that far. This bus would take him to the outer suburbs and in the direction he wanted to go. Without hesitation, Mowry jumped aboard.

Although his knowledge of the town was small, his inward journey had given him a good idea of how far he could go without reaching the fringes. A police check was likeliest just outside the town, where the road left the built-up area and ran through the country. At that point, all passengers could be regarded as leaving Alapertane and therefore fit subjects for questioning. He must get off the bus before then.

Dismounting in good time, he continued walking outward in the hope that, on foot, he could avoid the checking-post by taking to the fields. Day was almost done; the sun was half under the horizon, and light was dimming fast.

He slowed his pace, and decided that he'd stand a better chance of getting through in darkness. But he dared not draw attention to himself by strolling up and down the road, or sitting on the curb until nightfall. It was essential that he look like a local citizen homeward bound. Turning off the main road, he detoured through a long series of side roads, circled back, and regained the main one when the sky was black.

Continuing outward, he concentrated attention straight ahead. After a while, the road-lights ended; the shine from many house windows ceased, and in the distance he could see the sky-glow of the airport. It would be any time now; he had a strong urge to walk through the darkness on tiptoe.

A bus overtook him, hummed into the heavy gloom, and stopped with a brief blaze of braking lights. Cautiously, Mowry advanced to within twenty yards of the bus. It was fully loaded with passengers and luggage. Three policemen were on board; two of them checking faces and documents, while the third blocked the exit door.

On the verge, and right alongside James Mowry, stood a cruiser, its doors wide open and its lights extinguished. It would have been almost invisible had it not been for the glow from the nearby bus. But for the present holdup, he might have sneaked to within nabbing distance, before seeing it; they'd have sat in silence, listening to the faint scuffle of his feet, and jumped him as he came abreast of them.

Calmly he got into the cruiser, sat behind its wheel, closed the doors, and started the dynomotor. On the bus an irate cop was yelling at a frightened passenger, while his two fellows looked on with cynical amusement. The click of door-locks and the low whine of a motor went unheard during this stream of abuse.

Rolling the cruiser off the verge and onto the road, Mowry switched on the powerful headlights. Twin beams pierced the night, bathed a long stretch of road in shining amber, and filled the bus with their glare. He accelerated past the bus, saw the three cops and a dozen passengers staring out at him.

Mowry raced ahead, feeling that the fates had been kind and compensated for recent ill fortune. It was going to be some time before the alarm went out and the pursuit commenced. By the looks on the faces of those police, they had not realized that it was their own car shooting past. Perhaps they thought he was a motorist who'd taken advantage of their preoccupation to slip by unquestioned; if so, they might say nothing and do nothing about it, lest they earn reproof from their superiors.

But it was likely they'd take action to prevent a recurrence. Two of them would continue to browbeat the bus passengers while the third went out to catch any further sneaks.

That's when the fun would start. Mowry would give a lot to see their faces. No cruiser meant no radio, either; they'd have to rush the bus to the far-off airport, or stir their lazy legs and run like mad to the nearest house with a telephone. Better still, they'd have to make a humiliating confession over the line and take a verbal beating-up from the other end.

This mental reminder that in seizing the car he had also acquired a police radio spurred Mowry to switch it on. At once it came to life.

'Car Ten. Suspect claims he was examining parked cars because he's completely forgotten where he's left his own. He is unsteady, his speech is slurred, and he smells of *zith* – but he may be putting on an act.'

'Bring him in, Car Ten,' ordered Alapertane HQ.

Soon afterward, Car Nineteen asked for help in ringing a waterfront warehouse, reason not stated. Three cars were ordered to rush there at once.

Mowry turned the two-way switch to get the other channel. It was silent a long time before it said, 'K-car. Waltagan calling. A seventh has now entered house.'

A voice rasped back. 'You'd better wait. The other two may turn up yet.'

That sounded as if some unfortunate household was going to suffer a late-night raid by the Kaitempi. The motive was anyone's guess; the Kaitempi could and would snatch anyone for reasons known only to themselves; they could draft any citizen into the ranks of *DAG* merely by declaring him in.

He switched back to the police channel because over that would come the howl about a missing cruiser. The radio continued to mutter about suspects, fugitives, this, that or the other car, go here, go there and so forth. Mowry ignored the gab.

When twenty-five *den* from Alapertane, the radio yelped as the big long-range transmitter in Pertane itself let go with a powerful bellow, 'General call. Car Four stolen from Alapertane Police. Last seen racing south on main road to Valapan. May now be passing through area P6-P7.'

Replies came promptly from all cruisers within or near the designated area. There were eleven. The Pertane transmitter started moving them around like pieces on a chessboard, using coded map-references that meant nothing to the listener.

One thing seemed certain: if he kept to the main Valapan road, it wouldn't be long before a cruiser spotted him and drew every car within range to converge upon him. To take to minor roads and tracks wouldn't help any; they'd expect a trick like that and perhaps even now were taking steps to counter it.

He could ditch the car on the other side of a field, all its lights out, and take to foot – in which case they would not find it before daylight tomorrow. But unless he could grab another car, he'd be faced with a walk that would last all night, and all next day – perhaps longer if he was forced to take cover frequently.

Listening to the calls still coming over the air, and irritated by the mysterious map-references, it struck Mowry that this systematic concentration of the search was based on the supposition that if a suspect flees in a given direction at a given average speed he must be within a given area at a given time. This area had a radius plenty large enough to allow for turnoffs and detours. All they needed to do was bottle all the exits and then run along every road within the trap.

Suppose they did just that and found nothing? Ten to one, they'd jump to a couple of conclusions: the fugitive had never entered the area because he had reversed direction and now was racing northward; or else he had made far better speed than expected, had gone right through the district before the trap closed and now was southward of it. Either way, they'd remove the local pressure and switch the chase nearer to Valapan or northward of Alapertane.

He whizzed past a side road before he saw it, braked, reversed and went forward into it. A faint glow strengthened above a rise farther along the road he'd just left. Tearing along the badly rutted side road, while the distant glow sharpened in brilliance, he waited until the last moment before stopping and switching off his own lights.

In total darkness he sat there while a pair of blazing headlights came over the hill. Automatically his hand opened the door and he made ready to bolt if the lights should slow down and enter his own road.

The oncomer approached the junction and stopped.

James Mowry got out, stood by his car with gun held ready

and legs tensed. The next moment the other car surged forward along its own road, dimmed into the distance and was gone. There was no way of telling whether it had been a hesitant civilian or a police patrol. If the latter, they must have looked up the gloom-wrapped side road and seen nothing to tempt them into it. They'd get around to that in due time; finding nothing on the major roads, they'd eventually take to the minor ones.

Breathing heavily, Mowry got back behind the wheel, switched on his lights, and made good pace onward. Before long, he reached a farm and paused to look it over. Its yard and outbuildings adjoined the farmhouse, in which thin gleams of light showed the occupants to be still awake. Leaving the place, he pushed on.

He checked two more farms before finding one suitable to his purpose. The house stood in complete darkness and its barn was some distance from it. With dimmed lights, moving slowly and quietly, he drove through the muddy yard, along a narrow lane, and stopped under the open end of the barn. Leaving the car, he climbed atop the hay and lay there.

Over the next four hours the shine of distant headlights swept repeatedly all around. Twice a car rocked and plunged along the side road, and passed the farm without stopping. Both times he sat up in the hay and took out his gun. Evidently it did not occur to the hunters that he might park within the trap; on Jaimec, fugitives from the police or Kaitempi did not behave like that – given a head start, they kept running.

Gradually surrounding activity died down and ceased. Mowry got back into the cruiser and resumed his run. It was now three hours to dawn; if all went well, he'd make it to the rim of the forest before daybreak.

The Pertane transmitter was still broadcasting orders made incomprehensible by use of symbols, but the responses from various cruisers now came through with much less strength. He couldn't decide whether this fading of radio signals was an encouraging sign. It was certain that the transmitting cars were a good distance away, but there was no knowing how many might be nearer and maintaining silence. Knowing full well that he was able to listen in to their calls, the enemy was crafty enough to let some cars play possum.

Whether or not some cruisers were hanging around and saying nothing, he managed to get undetected to within nine *den* of his destination before the car gave up. It was tearing through a cutting that led to the last, dangerous stretch of main road when the green telltale light amid the instruments faded and went out. At the same time the headlamps extinguished and the radio died. The car rolled a short distance under its own momentum and stopped.

Examining the switch, Mowry could find nothing wrong with it. The emergency switch on the floorboard didn't work, either. After a good deal of fumbling in the dark, he managed to detach one of the intake leads and tried shorting it to the earth terminal. This should have produced a thin thread of blue light; it didn't.

It signified only one thing: the power-broadcast from the capital had been cut off. Every car within considerable radius of Pertane had been halted – police and Kaitempi cruisers included. Only vehicles within potency-range of other, faraway power transmitters could continue running – unless those also had ceased to radiate.

Leaving the car, Mowry started to trudge the rest of the way. He reached the main road, moved along it at a fast pace while keeping on the lookout for armed figures waiting ahead to challenge any pedestrian in the night.

After half an hour, a string of lights bloomed far behind him and to his ears came the muffled whine of many motors. Scrambling off the road, he fell into an unseen ditch, climbed out of it and sought refuge amid a bunch of low but thick bushes. The lights came nearer, shot past.

It was a military scout-patrol, twelve in number, mounted on dynocycles independently powered by long-term batteries. In his plastic suit, with goggles and duralumin helmet, each rider looked more like a deep-sea diver than a soldier; across the back of every trooper hung a riot gun with a big pan-shaped magazine.

Those in authority, he decided, must be more than merely irritated to stall all cars and let the army take over the hunt for the missing patrol-car and its occupant. Still, from their view-point they had good reason to go to such lengths. *Dirac Angestun Gesept* had claimed the execution of Sagramatholou; and who-ever had taken the agent's machine must be a real, genuine member of *DAG*. They wanted a real member in their hands at any cost.

He speeded up – running short stretches, reverting to a fast walk, then running again. Once he lay flat on his face in tall, fish-scented stuff that passed for grass on Jaimec. A patrol of six went by. Later he got behind a tree to avoid four more. To one side the sky had turned from black to gray, and visibility was improving every minute.

The last lap to the forest was the worst. In ten minutes he leaped for cover ten times, each time uncertain whether he had been seen – because now it was possible to observe movement over a considerable distance. This sudden increase in local activity suggested that the Alapertane patrol-car had been found – which meant they'd start seeking a fugitive on foot.

The chances were good that the searchers would not con-centrate on the immediate neighbourhood. Having no means of telling how long the car had been abandoned, they'd credit the fugitive with being four hours ahead of where he really was, and would probably look for him farther afield.

Thankfully he entered the forest, and made good time in growing daylight. Tired and hungry, James Mowry was com-pelled to rest ten minutes in every hour, but got along as fast as he could between times. By midday, when about an hour from the cave, he had to lie down in a leafy glade and snatch some sleep. Up to that point he had walked a total of thirty-seven Earth-miles helped by desperation, a sense of urgency, and Jaimec's lesser gravitation.

A little refreshed he resumed his journey and had reduced his pace to a listless amble when he reached the point where his finger-ring invariably began to tingle. This time it gave no response. He halted at once, looked all around, and studied the branches of big trees ahead. The forest was a maze of light and shadow. A silent, motionless sentinel could remain high up in a tree for hours and not be seen by anyone approaching.

What he'd been told at college echoed in his mind. 'The ring is a warning, a reliable alarm. Heed it!'

It was all very well, their saying that. It's one thing to give advice, something else to take it. The choice was not the simple one of going ahead or going back; it was that of finding shelter, food, comfort, and necessary equipment, or abandoning everything that enabled James Mowry to operate as a wasp. He hesitated, sorely tempted to sneak near enough at least to get a good, long look at the cave.

Finally he compromised by moving cautiously forward, edging from tree to tree and taking full advantage of all available cover. In this way he advanced another hundred yards.

There was still no response from the ring. Removing it from his ringer, he examined its sensitive crystal, cleaned the back of it, put it on again. Not an itch, not a twitch.

Half-hidden behind an enormous tree root, he again considered the position. Had there really been intruders in the cave and, if so, were they in ambush around it? Or had Container-22 ceased to function because of some internal defect?

While he stood there in an agony of indecision, a sound came from twenty yards ahead. Low and faint, he would never have heard it had his senses not been primed by peril. It was like a suppressed sneeze or a muffled cough. That was enough for him. *Someone* was hanging around and striving to keep quiet about it; the cave and its contents had been discovered and the finders were lying in wait for the owner to come along.

Trying to keep full attention on the trees, he backed away, almost at a crawl. After that, it took him an hour to make a mile; considering himself now at a safe distance, he broke into a steady walk, not knowing where to go or what to do.

Though speculation was futile, he could not help wondering how the cache had been found. Low-flying scout-planes fitted with supersensitive metal detectors could have pinpointed its exact location if they'd reason to suspect its existence in that area. But they'd had no such cause, so far as he was aware.

Most likely the cave had been stumbled upon by some of those who'd fled from Pertane and taken to the woods – they'd certainly curry favour with authority by reporting the find. Or perhaps the likely looking hide-out had been probed by an army patrol trying to round up refugees.

Anyway, it no longer mattered. He had lost the cache, as well as further contact with Terra. All that he possessed were the clothes in which he stood, a gun, and twenty thousand guilders. He was a rich man who owned nothing but his life, and that not worth much.

It was obvious that he must keep going away from the cave for as long as he retained strength to move. Realizing that they had found a Terran war-dump, the powers that be wouldn't long rest content with a mere ambush around it. Just as soon as they could collect the troops, they'd convert a large section of the forest into a gigantic trap; that process would start almost any time.

So, with stumbling legs, he kept going, steering himself by sun and shadow, maintaining his direction steadily south-east. By dusk he'd had as much as he could take; flopping into a patch of reeds, he closed his eyes and slept.

It was still dark when he awoke. He lay there until sunrise, dozing and waking at intervals. Then he started out with stronger legs, a fresher mind, but weaker insides.

FOURTEEN

Air activity was endless that day. Scout-planes and 'copters zoomed around within hearing distance all the time. The reason for all this display was a mystery, since they could have little hope of spotting one man in that immense forest. Perhaps the size of the cache had misled them into thinking that a Spakum task-force had landed.

It was easy to imagine the state of wild alarm in the capital, with brass hats running to and fro while messages flashed back and forth between Jaimec and Diracta. The two convicts Wolf had talked about had accomplished nothing like this. They'd tied up twenty-seven thousands for fourteen hours; by the looks of it, James Mowry would preoccupy the entire planet for the next fourteen weeks.

At nightfall, all the nourishment he had had was water, and his sleep was made restless with hunger. In the morning he continued through virgin forest that stretched all the way to the equator.

After five hours, he struck a narrow lane and followed it to a clearing in which were a small sawmill and a dozen cottages. Before the mill stood two powerful trucks. From the shelter of the trees he regarded them enviously. Nobody was near them at the moment; he could jump into either of them and tear away with no trouble at all. But the news of the theft would get the entire hunt on his trail. Right now, they had no idea of where he'd got to, or where he was heading. It was better to let their ignorance remain his bliss.

Snooping carefully between the trees, Mowry bided his time, bolted into a nearby garden, hurriedly filled his pockets with vegetables and his arms with fruit. Back among the trees he ate the fruit as he went along. Later, as twilight fell, he risked a small fire, baked the vegetables, ate half of them, and saved the rest for the morrow.

Next day he saw not a living soul and had no food except that reserved from yesterday. The day after that was worse: just trees, and still more trees, with not an edible nut or berry among the lot. From far to the north still came the faint humming of aircraft; that was the only thing to suggest the presence of life on the planet.

Four days later, he reached the side road to Elvera, a village south of Valapan. Still keeping to the trees, he followed it until houses came in sight. The amount of traffic on the road wasn't abnormal, and there were no signs of a special watch being kept.

By now he was in a bad way, haggard with lack of food, his clothing dirty and rumpled. It was fortunate, he thought, that he had darkened his complexion, that depilatory treatment had long abolished the need to shave, and that his last haircut had been the Halopti crop followed by imitation balding. Otherwise, he'd now look like nothing this side of Aldebaran.

He spent some time brushing his clothes with his hands and tidying himself as best he could. That done, he walked boldly into the village. If the price of a feed was a noose around the neck he was willing to pay it – provided the meal was a good one and that he was given time to draw his gun.

There were a dozen shops in the village, including a café bar of the kind favoured by truckers. Entering, he went straight through to the washroom, cleaned up, and saw himself in a mirror for the first time in many days. He looked sufficiently harassed to make a nosy cop give him the long, hard stare, but at least he wasn't an obvious hobo.

Returning to the front, he sat at the counter. The only other customers in the place were two ancient Sirians guzzling at one table, and too intent to bother with the newcomer. A burly

character in a white coat appeared behind the counter and
eyed Mowry with faint curiosity.

'You wish?'

Mowry told him, and got it. He set to, forcing himself to eat
slowly because the other was watching. Finishing, he ordered
the next item and disposed of it in the same bored manner.

As he shoved across the final drink, the burly one said,
'Come far?'

'Only from Valapan.'

'Walk it, *hi?*'

'Nar, the dyno stalled two *den* back. I'll fix it after.'

The other stared at him. 'You came in a dyno? How'd you
get out of Valapan?'

'What d'you mean?' countered Mowry.

'No cars allowed into or out of Valapan today. A cop told
me so himself.'

'When was this?'

'Around the nine-time hour.'

'I was away before seven,' Mowry said. 'I'd a lot of calls to
make and got out early. Good thing I did, *hi?*'

'Yar,' agreed the other doubtfully. 'But how're you going to
get in again?'

'I don't know. They've got to lift the ban sometime; they
can't maintain it forever.' He paid the bill, made for the door.
'Live long.'

He sensed that he'd gotten out of there in good time. The
burly one was vaguely suspicious, but not sufficiently so to bawl
for help; he was the type who'd hesitate lest he make a fool of
himself.

The next call was at a nearby grocery store. He bought
enough of the most concentrated foods to make a package
not too heavy to carry for miles. Here he was served without
especial interest, and the conversation was brief.

'Bad about Valapan, isn't it?'

'Yar,' said Mowry, yearning to hear the news.

'Hope they nab every stinking Spakum in the place.'

'Yar,' Mowry repeated.

'Damn the Spakums!' the other finished. 'That will be sixteen and six-tenths.'

Going out with the package, he glanced along the road. The fellow at the café-bar was standing by his door looking at him. Mowry nodded familiarly, ambled from the village, shot another glance back as he passed the last house. Nosypoke was still standing there watching him.

With careful rationing, the food lasted him ten days as he continued through the forest and saw nobody other than occasional lumberjacks whom he avoided. His direction was now a westward circle that should bring him not far south of Radine. Despite any risks entailed, he was keeping to that part of Jaimec of which he had some knowledge.

He'd made up his mind that when he got near to Radine he was going to use his gun to acquire another car and a set of genuine documents, even if he had to bury a corpse in the woods. After that, he'd check the lay of the land; if things weren't too hot in Radine, maybe he could hole-up there. Something drastic had to be done, because he could not roam the forests forever. If he'd acquired the status of a lone outlaw, he might as well become enough of a bandit to prosper.

Two hours after sunset, on his last day of wandering, James Mowry reached the main Radine-Khamasta road, paralleled it through the forest as he continued toward Radine. At precisely the eleven-time hour, a tremendous flash of light yellowed the sky in the direction of the stronghold of Khamasta. Beneath his feet, the ground gave a distinct quiver; the trees creaked while their tops swayed. A bit later a prolonged, faraway growl came over the horizon.

Traffic on the road swiftly thinned out and finally ceased altogether. A thousand crimson serpents hissed up from darkened Radine and hungrily bored into the night sky. Came another great flash from the region of Khamasta. Something long, black, and noisy bulleted low over the forest, moment-arily blanking out the stars and sending down a blast of heat.

In the distance, he heard faint, muffled rumblings, crack-lings, thumps and thuds, plus a vague, indefinable babble like the shoutings of a multitude. Mowry went into the empty road and stared up at the sky. The stars vanished wholesale as the thrice-wrecked and ten-times-decimated Terran fleets thun-dered overhead four thousand strong.

Below, Mowry danced like a maniac in the middle of the road. He shouted at the sky; he yelled and screamed and bawled tuneless songs with meaningless words. He waved his arms around, and tossed twenty thousand guilders into the air so that they floated around like confetti.

As the black, snouty warships roared above, a veritable torrent of stuff sailed down, seeking ground with the pale, lemon-coloured legs of antigrav beams. He stood fascinated while not far away a huge, cumbersome shape with enormous caterpillar tracks fell featherlike atop twenty columnar rays, and landed with squeaks of protest from big springs.

Heart pounding, he tore southward along the road, on and on until he bolted full tilt into a waiting group of forty figures. They were looking his way, ready for him, having been alerted by the frantic clomping of his feet. The entire bunch topped him by head and shoulders, wore dark green uniforms and were holding things that gleamed in the starlight.

'Take it easy, Blowfly,' advised a Terran voice.

Mowry panted for breath. He did not resent this rude counterthrust to the Spakum tag. Every Sirian was a blowfly by virtue of his purple backside. He pawed at the speaker's sleeve. 'My name is James Mowry. I'm not what I seem – I'm a Terran.'

The other, a big lean-faced, and cynical sergeant, said, 'My name's Napoleon, I'm not what I seem – I'm an emperor.' He gestured with a hand holding a whop-gun that looked like a cannon. 'Take him to the cage, Rogan.'

'But I *am* a Terran,' yelped Mowry, flapping his hands.

'Yeah, you look it,' said the sergeant.

'I'm *speaking* Terran.'

'Sure are. A hundred thousand Blowflies can speak it. They think it gives them a certain something.' He waved the cannon again. 'The cage, Rogan.'

Rogan took him.

For twelve days he ambled around the prisoner-of-war compound. The place was very big, very full, and swiftly became fuller. Prisoners were fed regularly, and guarded constantly; that was all.

Of his fellows behind the wire, at least fifty sly-eyed specimens boasted of their confidence in the future when the sheep would be sorted from the goats and justice would be done. The reason, they asserted, was that for a long time they'd been secret leaders of *Dirac Angestun Gesept* and undoubtedly would be raised to power when Terran conquerors got around to it. Then, they warned, friends would be rewarded as surely as foes would be punished. This bragging ceased only when three of them somehow got strangled in their sleep.

At least a dozen times Mowry seized the chance to attract the attention of a patrolling sentry when no Sirian happened to be nearby. 'Psst! My name's Mowry – I'm a Terran.'

Ten times he received confessions of faith such as, 'You look it!' or 'Is zat *so?*'

A lanky character said, 'Don't give me that!'

'It's true – I swear it!'

'You really are a Terran – *hi?*'

'Yar,' said Mowry, forgetting himself.

'Yar to you, too.'

Once he spelled it so there'd be no possibility of misunderstanding. 'See here. Buster, I'm a T-E-R-R-A-N.'

To which the sentry replied 'Says Y-O-U,' and hefted his gun and continued his patrol.

Came the day when prisoners were paraded in serried ranks, a captain stood on a crate, held a loud-hailer before his mouth and roared all over the camp, 'Anyone here named James Mowry?'

Mowry galloped eagerly forward, bowlegged from force of habit. 'I am.' He scratched himself, a performance that the captain viewed with unconcealed disfavour.

Glowering at him, the captain demanded, 'Why haven't you said so before now? We've been searching all Jaimec for you. Let me tell you, Mister, we've got better things to do. You struck dumb or something?'

'I . . .'

'Shut up! Military Intelligence wants you. Follow me.'

So saying, he led the other through heavily guarded gates, along a path toward a prefab hut.

Mowry ventured, 'Captain, again and again I tried to tell the sentries that . . .'

'Prisoners are forbidden to talk to sentries,' the captain snapped.

'But I wasn't a prisoner.'

'Then what the blazes were you doing in there?' Without waiting for a reply, he pushed open the door of the prefab hut and introduced Mowry with, 'This is the bum.'

The intelligence officer glanced up from a wad of papers. 'So you're Mowry, James Mowry?'

'Correct.'

'Well now,' said the officer, 'we've been primed by beam-radio and we know all about you.'

'Do you really?' responded Mowry, pleased and gratified. He braced himself for the coming citation.

'Another mug like you was on Artishain, their tenth planet,' the officer went on. 'Fellar named Kingsley. They say he hasn't sent a signal for quite a piece. Looks like he's got himself nabbed.'

Mowry said suspiciously, 'What's this to me?'

'We're dropping you in his place. You leave tomorrow.'

'*Hi?* Tomorrow?'

'Sure thing. We want you to become a wasp. Nothing wrong with you, is there?'

'No,' said Mowry, very feebly. 'Only my head.'

Eric Frank Russell was born in Berkshire in 1905. He was the first British writer to contribute regularly to *Astounding Science Fiction*, his first story, 'The Saga of Pelican West', appearing in that magazine in 1937. His novels include *Sinister Barrier*, *Wasp* and *The Great Explosion* and his short fiction has appeared in a number of collections. He died in 1978.

A full list of SF Masterworks can be found at

www.gollancz.co.uk